Jacob

The Florence Stories

Jacob Abbott

The Florence Stories

Reprint of the original, first published in 1861.

1st Edition 2022 | ISBN: 978-3-37505-718-3

Verlag (Publisher): Salzwasser Verlag GmbH, Zeilweg 44, 60439 Frankfurt, Deutschland
Vertretungsberechtigt (Authorized to represent): E. Roepke, Zeilweg 44, 60439 Frankfurt, Deutschland
Druck (Print): Books on Demand GmbH, In de Tarpen 42, 22848 Norderstedt, Deutschland

THE

FLORENCE STORIES,

BY JACOB ABBOTT.

EXCURSION TO THE ORKNEY ISLANDS.

NEW YORK:
SHELDON & COMPANY,
115 NASSAU STREET.

1861.

LANDING AT BEN NEVIS.

ENGRAVINGS.

		PAGE
I.—LANDING AT BEN NEVIS		Frontispiece.
II.—CHOOSING THE STATE ROOMS		23
III.—VISIT TO THE ORKNEY ISLANDS		97
IV.—ON BOARD THE IONA		127
V.—CROSSING THE MICKLE FERRY		195
VI.—THE BLACK CRAIGS		225

CONTENTS.

CHAPTER	PAGE
I.—Letter from Singapore	11
II.—Taking Passage	15
III.—Preparations	21
IV.—The Letter of Credit	36
V.—The Embarkation	51
VI.—Life on board Ship	61
VII.—Morning in Liverpool	80
VIII.—Plans Formed	87
IX.—The Railway Ride	107
X.—The Highland Glens	122
XI.—Ben Nevis	135
XII.—The Caledonian Canal	153
XIII.—The Vitrified Fort	172
XIV.—Night Ride by Daylight	188
XV.—The Prince Consort	200
XVI.—Kirkwall	212
XVII.—The Stones of Stennis	222
XVIII.—The Embarkation	234
XIX.—Conclusion	249

THE ORKNEY ISLANDS.

CHAPTER I.

LETTER FROM SINGAPORE.

On one occasion, when Mrs. Morelle went down to New York with Grimkie and her two children Florence and John, while her husband was in the East Indies, she heard that a letter had arrived from him that very day, and that it had just been sent to the post-office in order to be conveyed to her at her house up the North River. The letter, she was told, came from Singapore.

Singapore is a large English port situated just about half way round the world from America, on the way to the East Indies. It is a sort of center and rendezvous for all ships navigating those seas, and letters go and come to and from it in all directions.

It is often visited, moreover, by ships of war, cruising in those seas.

Grimkie went down to New York with his aunt and cousins, on this occasion, because it was holiday at his school at the Chateau. Every Saturday was holiday at the Chateau.

His aunt and also his cousins were always very glad to have him go to New York with them when they went, but he never left his school to go on such excursions, except upon the regular holidays.

Mrs. Morelle would have been very impatient to reach home if she had supposed that her husband's letter would arrive there before she did. But she knew very well that the mail from New York did not get in till about eight o'clock, and that the letter would not be brought up to the Octagon until about half-past eight. She was, therefore, not in any special haste to reach the end of the voyage, but amused herself talking with the children very quietly and contentedly all the way.

The steamboat arrived between four and five. Grimkie obtained a carriage at the pier, and, after assisting Mrs. Morelle and the children to get into it, he bade them good-by, and turned his own steps toward the Chateau.

At half-past eight o'clock the letter came. Mrs. Morelle, who had been watching for the coming of the boy who brought the mail, took the letter from him at the door, and went at once into her little room to read it. It was as follows:

SINGAPORE, August 16.

"MY VERY DEAR WIFE:

"I have just arrived at this port from Calcutta, on my way to Canton, and in consequence of letters which I have received here I find that next summer I shall have occasion to go to London. I hope to reach there about the first of September.

"Now I have a plan to propose to you, though I do not know what you will think of it. It is no less than this—that you should take the children and come out to England and meet me. I shall be able to spend four or five weeks in England, and then I must return to Canton again. I might come to America in that time to see you, instead of asking you to cross the Atlantic to see me, but if I were to do so, the voyage would occupy nearly all the time that I should have to spare, and thus leave me only a very few days to spend in your company; whereas, if you come to London, I can enjoy the pleasure of being with you and the children a whole month.

"Besides, I think it might perhaps be agreeable to you, and also improving to the children, to make a little tour in England and France.

The facilities for travelling are such now that I think you will have no difficulty in coming out alone. If you approve of this plan, I would recommend to you to cross early in June, and spend a little time in rambling about England before I come. By sending your address to my bankers from time to time, I could come to you immediately on my arrival. Let me know what you think of this plan.

"The overland mail is just closing, so I can not write any more at this time, I shall, however, write you again very soon, and in the meantime I am your very affectionate husband.

JAMES MORELLE."

The children came into the room just as their mother had finished reading her letter, and so she read it aloud to them. They were very much excited at the idea of making a voyage to England, and they asked their mother if she thought she would go.

"Yes," said Mrs. Morelle. "I *rather* think I shall."

The children clapped their hands with delight at hearing this answer.

"I wish that Grimkie could go with us," said Florence.

"So do I," said John.

"Ah!" responded Mrs. Morelle, shaking her head, "I am afraid that will be impossible."

CHAPTER II.

TAKING PASSAGE.

WHILE Mrs. Morelle was reflecting upon the arrangements which she should make for her intended voyage, she thought a great deal of the suggestion which Florence had made, namely, that she should take Grimkie with her.

"I wish I *could* take him with me," said she. "He would be a great help to me, and a great reliance. He is so capable, and at the same time so considerate; besides, he would be a great deal of company for the children, and would make the tour not only doubly pleasant, but doubly profitable for them."

But then there was the difficulty of his studies. He was fitting for college; and Mrs. Morelle knew very well that his father was always extremely unwilling to allow any thing to interfere with his studies in school.

At first, Mrs. Morelle thought that this difficulty was insurmountable, and that it was wholly out of the question that Grimkie should accompany them on the proposed tour. But on reflecting more fully upon the subject, she recollected that it was not usually considered well for a boy to enter college until he was about sixteen years of age, whereas Grimkie was not yet fourteen. She knew also that he was already pretty nearly fitted for college, and she thought it possible that his father might think that he could now spare a year from his studies as well as not. It would undoubtedly be greatly promotive of his health, she thought, and of the strength of his constitution, to spend a year in travelling, and thus enable him to enter upon his college course with more vigor and energy. He might travel with her and the children a year, she thought, and still leave a year for school, to complete his preparations for the college examination, before it would be time for him to be offered.

So she determined to propose the plan to Grimkie's father, though she did it with great doubt and hesitation.

"It will be exactly what I want for him," said Mr. Jay, when he heard the proposal. "I have been quite at a loss to decide what to do with him for the two coming years. I thought seriously of sending him to some farmer for a year. A boy ought not to be kept at his studies all the time, while he is growing.

"But it seems to me, sister," he added, after a moment's pause, "that you show a great deal of courage in undertaking the charge of three such children, in making the tour of Europe. I should think your own two children would be charge enough for you."

"That is just it," said Mrs. Morelle. "They are too much of a charge, and so I want Grimkie to go with us to help me take care of them."

Mr. Jay made no farther objection, and so it was arranged that Grimkie should go.

Mr. Jay made it a condition, however, that Grimkie should have all the charge of the baggage and of the accounts during the tour, so as to learn to do such business properly.

Grimkie was, of course, greatly pleased when he heard of the plan which had thus been formed for him, and it was determined that the very next Saturday the whole party should go to New York and take passage in the Cunard line of steamers. It was necessary for Grimkie to go, for this was a part of the business which he was bound to attend to, according to the arrangement. Grimkie wished that Mrs. Morelle should go, in order that she might choose the staterooms which the party were to occupy, and Florence and John must go for the pleasure of being of the party.

"Besides," said Florence, "we want to go on board the ship and see the staterooms."

"Ah! but we are not going on board the ship," replied Grimkie: "we are only going to the office."

"Then how is mother going to choose the staterooms that we are to have," said Florence, "if she does not see them."

"She will see a plan of them," said Grimkie. "They have plans of all the ships at the office, with the plans and shapes of all the staterooms laid down upon them."

"Ho!" said John, in a tone of disappointment; "I don't care any thing about seeing a plan. Nevertheless," he added, after a moment's pause, "I should like to go."

So it was agreed that they should all go together.

It was necessary to go immediately, too; for the berths and staterooms in the Atlantic steamers are usually engaged long beforehand. Mrs. Morelle asked Grimkie to inquire which was the best steamer in the Cunard line; for as the precise time of their sailing was not material, they could go a little sooner or later, for the sake of having one of the best ships.

Grimkie accordingly inquired, and he learned that the *Persia* was the largest of the ships, though in other respects they were all nearly equally good. Mrs. Morelle accordingly determined to take passage in the *Persia*, provided she found that that ship was going at any time near the first of June.

Accordingly, on the first Saturday morning after it was concluded that Grimkie should go, the whole party set out together to go to New York to engage the passages. They went down by the railroad, and arrived at the Chambers-street station about ten o'clock.

"This is just right," said Grimkie. "The office opens at ten, I suppose."

So Grimkie selected a nice looking carriage from among those that were standing at the station, and after assisting his aunt and his cousins to enter it, and also getting in himself, he directed the coachman to drive to the office of the Cunard Company. The office was situated at the foot of Broadway, opposite the lower end of the Bowling Green.

They all descended from the carriage, and went up the steps which led to the office. On entering it they found a large room, in the front part of which was a counter with a desk at one end of it, and on the counter were lying one or two immense books containing plans. The books were about a yard long, and perhaps two feet wide, and each leaf contained a plan. The leaves were very stiff, as if the plans had been pasted upon sheets of pasteboard, in order that they might be turned over easily, and also to protect them from injury by constant handling.

In the back part of the room were other desks, where several clerks were engaged in writing.

Grimkie accosted the clerk who stood at the desk near the counter, saying,.

"We came, sir, to engage passages in one of your ships."

The clerk bowed politely to Mrs. Morelle, and after some conversation in respect to the time when she wished to sail, and the steamer which she preferred, he looked into his books, and found that the *Persia* would be coming to America, instead of going to Europe, about the first of June; also that the ship which would sail from New York nearest to that time, namely, on the 23d of May, was full. All the staterooms were engaged. There were, however, some excellent staterooms at liberty in the Boston steamer, which sailed on the following week, namely, the 30th of May.

And here, perhaps, it is necessary to explain that there are two branches to the Cunard line of steamers, one of which connects Liverpool with Boston, and the other with New York. A

Taking Passage.

ship of each line sails alternately from Boston and New York—one week from Boston, and the next from New York.

As soon as Grimkie heard that there were good staterooms disengaged in the Boston steamer of the 30th of May, his eye brightened up at once, and he proposed that they should go that way.

"But that will make us an extra journey from here to Boston," said Mrs. Morelle.

"Yes, Auntie," said Grimkie, "that is just the thing. We shall have the journey to Boston into the bargain, and without paying anything for it, for the price is less from Boston, and a good deal more than enough less to pay the expenses of going."

"Yes, mother," said Florence, "let us go that way."

"Besides," said Grimkie, "the Boston steamers touch at Halifax, into the bargain."

"Is that so?" said Mrs. Morelle, turning to the clerk.

"Yes, madam," said the clerk, smiling; "but I think the passengers do not usually consider the touching at Halifax any special advantage in favor of the Boston line."

"Why? Does not the ship stop long enough for them to go on shore?" asked Mrs. Morelle.

"She stops usually two or three hours," replied the clerk; "and the passengers can go ashore, if they please."

"Then let us go that way, mother," said Florence.

"We *must* go that way for aught I see," said Mrs. Morelle, "if there are no staterooms for us in the New York steamers."

The clerk looked into his books again, and said that there were no two continuous staterooms disengaged in the New York steamers until after the middle of June. He, however, then opened one of the big books, and showed Mrs. Morelle the plan of the *Europa*, which was the Boston steamer that was to sail on the 30th, and pointed out upon the plan two staterooms lying contiguous to each other, which were disengaged.

One of them was what was called the family stateroom, being nearly square in form, with two berths, one over the other, at the end, and a settee along the side, upon which a third person might sleep, if necessary.

"I could sleep on the sofa, mother," said John, "just as well as not."

"Then what should we do with Grimkie," asked Mrs. Morelle.

"We might give the young gentleman a sep-

CHOOSING THE STATE ROOMS.

arate berth in another stateroom," said the clerk; "and then you would have only three passages to pay for. But in that case," added the clerk, "you might find it more convenient to let the young lady sleep upon the sofa, as the upper berth is pretty high, and her brother could climb up to it perhaps more easily than she could."

"*I* can climb," said John, eagerly. "I can climb up to the upper berth, just as well as not."

Mrs. Morelle found, on further conversation with the clerk, that if she took only a single berth in the second stateroom, the other berth would be occupied by some stranger, who might or might not be very agreeable company for Grimkie. So she concluded to take two staterooms herself, with a view of letting Grimkie and John occupy one of them, while she and Florence occupied the other. The clerk accordingly put down her name for two staterooms contiguous to each other, one of the large ones for herself and Florence, and a smaller one, next to it, for Grimkie and John. Mrs. Morelle paid the money and took a receipt, and then the whole party left the office and returned to the carriage.

CHAPTER III.

PREPARATIONS.

MANY weeks intervened between the time when Mrs. Morelle took her passage and the day appointed for sailing. During this interval all parties were very much occupied with making the various preparations necessary for such a tour. Mrs. Morelle bought three trunks all alike and of medium size. One of these trunks was for herself, one for Florence and John, and one for Grimkie.

These trunks were all of a medium size, that is, about as large as could be conveniently handled when full, by one man. Mrs. Morelle had learned by former experience in travelling in Europe, that occasions would often occur when it was very inconvenient to have a trunk which it required two men to lift and carry away.

Besides these trunks Mrs. Morelle bought a sort of valise as large as she thought Grimkie could conveniently carry in his hand, which contained a set of night dresses and certain toilet conveniences for the whole party. This she called the night valise.

"Because you see," she said in explaining the arrangement to Florence, "we are liable sometimes to be separated from our trunks for a night, but this valise we can keep with us at all times. Besides we shall sometimes wish to make a little excursion off from our main route, to be gone only a single night, and then we shall not wish to take our trunks with us. In such cases as this the night valise will be very convenient. Then it will be just the thing for me to use as a stool to put my feet upon in the railway carriages."

"I do'nt see how we can ever get separated from our trunks," said Florence. "They will always go with us in the same train."

"But accidents happen," said her mother. "In travelling, we have not only to make arrangements for the ordinary course of things, but we must also provide for accidents."

"What kind of accidents?" asked Florence.

"Every kind that you can imagine," said Mrs. Morelle.

"But tell me of one kind, mother," said Florence.

"At one time," replied Mrs. Morelle, "your father and I arrived in Liverpool late in the evening. It was eleven o'clock before we got through the custom-house. The ship could not go into dock because the tide was so low. So we were obliged to go ashore in a tender, which is a small steamer somewhat like a Brooklyn ferry-boat, but not half so large. It was dark and rainy, and the wind was blowing a heavy gale. We had to go down a long black ladder from the steamer to the tender. One of the officers of the ship held a lantern at the top, and a sailor held one below. We wished to take our trunks with us, but they said we could not do that. We must say what hotel we were going to, and they would send them there.

"So we told them that we were going to the Waterloo Hotel, and they marked all our trunks with a big W in chalk.

"Then we went down the ladder to the tender, and were sent on shore. When we landed we took a cab, and drove to the Waterloo Hotel. But we found that we could not have rooms there, for the hotel was full. So we were obliged to go to another and another. We went to three before we could get in.

"It was now about midnight, and we were very tired, and we would have liked very much to go to bed. If we had had night dresses with us we might have gone to bed at once, and let our trunks remain at the Waterloo until morning. But we had nothing of the kind, and so your father had to take a cab and go back to the Waterloo and wait there till the trunks came, and he did not get to our hotel so that we could undress and go to bed till nearly two o'clock."

"That was curious," said John, who had been standing by all the time, listening to the conversation. "But I don't understand very well what you mean about not getting into the docks."

"Ah, you'll find out all about that," said his mother, "when you get to Liverpool."

"Tell us some more accidents, then, mother," said John.

"No," said his mother. "I can not tell you of any more, but you will experience plenty of them, you may depend, if we travel about much in Europe, before we meet father."

One of the most important things to be arranged in making a tour in Europe is the question of funds. We can not take American money with us, for American money is not known, and does not circulate in foreign countries. We must have for each country which we wish to travel through, the kind of money that belongs to that country, except that in some cases we can use the money of a neighboring country, when it happens to be well known. We can use the principal gold coins of England and France, namely, the sovereign and the Napoleon, almost all over Europe, for they are almost universally known. With the exception of these, we require always the money of the country which we are travelling in.

Besides this, even if American money would circulate in foreign countries, it would be very inconvenient to take a sufficient quantity of it for a long tour, on account of the weight of it. I speak now, of course, of real money, that is, of gold or silver coin. Bank bills, as doubtless most of the readers of this book are aware, are not in fact money, but only the promises of banks to pay money. They pass as money in the country where the bank issuing them is situated, because every one knows that he can go with them to the bank and get the coin—that is, if he thinks the bank is good, and that it will keep its promises. But in foreign countries, where of course the banks issuing the bills are beyond the reach of the holders, the bills would be good for nothing except to sell at a loss to somebody who could send them across the Atlantic, and make arrangements for having the coin sent back to him.

The arrangements for furnishing travellers

with the money they require, are made by the great banking houses. The *banking houses* must not be confounded with the banks. They are private establishments, conducted by men of great wealth. They have branches of their establishments in all the great cities and towns in Europe and America, and large supplies of money at all of them. At each branch they have money of the country where the branch is situated. An American traveller going to Europe, can go accordingly to one of these banking houses in New York, and make arrangements there to be furnished with any amount of money at any of the great towns in Europe, and of such kinds as they require, on condition of repaying the value of it in American money in New York, as soon as the news of its having been paid can come over.

The document which the banker in New York gives to the traveller, instructing the branches in Europe to pay him the money he may require, is called a letter of credit. A letter of credit may be given for any sum of money, and continue in force for any period of time.

There are several precautions and conditions to be attended to in making arrangements for a letter of credit. In the first place, the banker requires some security that the money which is advanced to the traveller in foreign lands, will be promptly repaid to him in America, as soon as notice arrives in this country of his having received it. This security is given in various ways. Sometimes the traveller knows some responsible merchant in New York, who will guarantee that the money will be paid. When he does not know any such person, or does not wish to ask any person to become surety for him, he can deposit bank stock, or railway stock, or bonds, or any other sure and good titles to property which he happens to have, and give the banker authority to sell them, and pay himself with the proceeds, in case the traveller fails to make other provision for the repayment of the money advanced to him.

Another precaution which it is necessary to take, is one to prevent any other person than the traveller himself from getting any money with the letter of credit, in case he should steal it, or in any other way get it into his possession. Otherwise, in case the letter should be lost, and any dishonest person should find it, or in case it should be stolen, the wrongful holder of it might go with it to one of the bankers in foreign countries and ask for some money, and thus either the banker or the traveller would be robbed.

To prevent this, it is customary for the banker

to send specimens of the traveller's hand-writing to all the branches in Europe where the traveller thinks he shall wish to draw money. The traveller writes his name on several slips of paper, and the banker in New York sends one of the slips to each of the branches in Europe, where the traveller thinks he may wish to procure money. The clerks at these branches, when they receive these slips, which are sent to them by mail, paste them into a big book with a great many other slips of the same kind received before. Then, when the traveller arrives and calls for his money, they write a paper for him to sign, directing the person in New York who is to do the business for him there, to pay the amount to the banker in New York as soon as the paper reaches him. This paper is called a draft. When the traveller has signed the draft, the clerk at the branch in Europe takes it to the big book, and compares the signature with the one upon the slip of paper which he had received by mail. If he finds the hand-writing is the same, then he knows that all is right, and he pays the money. If it is not the same, then he knows that the person who has called with the letter of credit is not the person he pretends to be, and so he sends out at once for a police officer, and has him taken into custody.

In respect to the security to be lodged with the banker for the letter of credit, Grimkie had nothing to do, the merchants who had charge of Mrs. Morelle's funds having made arrangements for it; but Mr. Jay wished that Grimkie should attend to the business of procuring the letter himself, in order that he might learn how to do business at a banker's, and he recommended that Mrs. Morelle should go with him, so as to see how the business was done, and also to give specimens of her signature.

"You might write the specimens at home," he said, "and send them to the banker's; but I think it is a little better for you to go to the office. I could go with you just as well as not, but if you go alone you will see how easily the business is done, and you will have more confidence and self-possession in going to the banking houses in Europe. So I think I had better not go with you, but leave you altogether to Grimkie's care.

Mrs. Morelle entirely approved this arrangement; and, accordingly, on the morning of the day before she was to set out for Boston, she went with Grimkie and obtained the letter. It was on Monday that she did this. She had left her home on the North River the Saturday before, with a view of spending Sunday in New

York, and then, after attending to this and some other business in New York on Monday, of proceeding to Boston on Tuesday, so as to be ready to sail in the steamer on Wednesday, that being the appointed day.

How Grimkie succeeded in doing the business at the banker's, will appear in the next chapter.

CHAPTER IV.

THE LETTER OF CREDIT.

PERSONS who are not much accustomed to travelling, or to doing business for themselves in strange places, sometimes feel a good deal of solicitude when called upon to act in such cases, from not knowing beforehand exactly what they are to do. But there is never any occasion for such solicitude. It is not at all necessary when you have occasion to go to a bank, or to an office of any kind, or to a railway-station where a great many different trains are coming and going, that you should know beforehand what you are to do when you get there. All that is necessary is that you should simply know *what you want*, and that you should be able to state it intelligibly. It is the business of the clerks, or of the persons in charge of the establishment, whatever it may be, to show you how the business is to be done, when you once tell them what it is.

It was about eleven o'clock on Monday morning that Grimkie was to set out with Mrs. Morelle to go and get the letter of credit.

Florence and John were to go too, as they did not wish to be left at the hotel, but they were to remain in the carriage while Grimkie and his aunt went into the office.

Grimkie's father was at the hotel at the time that they set out.

"Now, Grimkie," said he, while Mrs. Morelle was putting on her bonnet and shawl, "do you know where you are going?"

"Yes, sir," said Grimkie, "you gave me the address of the banker, and I have got it in my pocket."

"Very good," said his father.

"And now do you know how to do the business when you get there?"

"No, sir," said Grimkie.

"Very good again," said his father. "It is not necessary that you should know how to do the business. It is not your duty to know. It is the duty of the clerks there to do the business for you. But do you know what the business is that you wish to have done?"

"Yes, sir," said Grimkie. "To get a letter of credit."

"In whose name?" asked his father.

"Mrs. Jane Morelle's," said Grimkie.

"For how much?" asked his father.

"For five hundred pounds," said Grimkie.

"How long to run?" asked his father.

"For one year," said Grimkie.

"Very good," said his father. "That is all you want to know. And remember, in all your travels, that if you have any business to do of any kind, in any strange place, all that is necessary for you is to know distinctly what you want, and to be able to state it intelligibly. The people of the establishment will attend to all the rest."

"Yes, sir," said Grimkie. "I will remember it."

Mrs. Morelle, who had been standing before the glass putting on her bonnet and shawl during this conversation, listened to it with much interest, and she felt great satisfaction and relief in hearing it. She had very naturally felt some uneasiness and apprehension in setting out upon such a tour, at the thought of being called upon often, as she knew she must be, at railway stations, and public offices of various kinds, to transact business without knowing at all how the business was to be done.

But if all that is necessary in such places, she said to herself, is that I should know what I want, and be able to state it intelligibly, I think I shall get along very well.

In fact, Grimkie's father meant what he said

much more for Mrs. Morelle than for Grimkie. He knew very well that boys of Grimkie's age were not usually very diffident, or distrustful of themselves, in regard to the transaction of business of any kind, and that they did not usually stand in need of any special encouragement.

When Grimkie entered the banking-house where he was to procure the letter, he was at first somewhat abashed by the scene which presented itself to view. He saw a very large room with doors opening in various directions into other rooms, all full of desks, and clerks, and people going and coming. There was a long counter with high desks, surmounted by little balustrades rising above it, and open spaces here and there, where people were receiving money, or delivering papers, or transacting other business. Grimkie was for a moment quite bewildered, but after a moment's hesitation he recalled to mind the instructions which he had received, and he went boldly up to the clerk who was nearest to him and said,

"I came to see about a letter of credit."

"Second desk to the right," said the clerk, pointing with his pen, but without raising his eyes from his work.

Grimkie, followed by Mrs. Morelle, went in the direction indicated. The desk was a very large and handsome one, and an elderly gentleman of very respectable appearance was sitting at it writing a letter. He went on with his work, but in a moment, glancing his eye at Grimkie, he said,

"Well, my son?"

"I came to see about a letter of credit," said Grimkie.

"What name?" asked the gentleman.

"Mrs. Jane Morelle," replied Grimkie.

"Ah!" said the gentleman, and looking up from his work his eye fell upon Mrs. Morelle, whom he now for the first time saw. He immediately rose from his seat and offered Mrs. Morelle a chair.

"It is all arranged about your letter of credit," said he, as he resumed his seat, "except to take your signatures. You will only wish to draw in London and Paris, I understand?"

"Yes, sir," said Mrs. Morelle. "Mr. Jay thought that that would be all that we should require."

The gentleman then called to a handsome-looking young clerk who was writing at a desk near by, and asked him if he would be kind enough to take Mrs. Morelle's signature. So the clerk conducted her to a table at a little distance, near a window, where there were writing materials, and asked her to write her name three or four times, at some little distance apart, upon a sheet of paper which he gave her. Grimkie followed his aunt to the table, and the clerk, after having given the directions, went away and left Mrs. Morelle to write at her leisure.

"I'm all in a trepidation," said Mrs. Morelle, taking the pen, "and it won't be written well."

"That will be just right, then, Auntie," said Grimkie, "for you will be all in a trepidation when you go to draw the money in the foreign cities, and so the writing will be the same."

Mrs. Morelle smiled, and then proceeded to write her name four times, in a column on the left hand side of the paper, each signature being at the distance of two inches from the other.

By the time that she had finished writing, the clerk came and took the paper. He then said to her that if she would remain seated a few minutes, he would bring the letter of credit to her.

Accordingly, in a few minutes he returned, bringing with him a letter folded and enclosed in a very strong envelope. Mrs. Morelle took the envelope, and then bowing to the clerk, and also to the gentleman at the desk, she and Grimkie retired.

As soon as they had returned to the hotel, Grimkie was curious to open the letter of credit and read it. He found that it was a handsomely printed form, covering one side of a sheet of letter paper, with the blanks filled up by a pen. It was as follows :

"NEW YORK, *May* 28, 1860.
"*Messrs. de Rothschild Brothers, Paris.*
"*Messrs. N. M. Rothschild and Son, London.*

"*Gentlemen:*

"This letter will be presented to you by *Mrs. Jane Morelle*, in whose favor we beg to open a credit with you collectively, for the sum of £500—*say Five Hundred Pounds*, to which extent be pleased to furnish payments in sums as required, without deduction, and against receipts, inscribing the amounts paid on the reverse of this letter, and reimbursing yourselves in accordance with our letter of advice, transmitting receipts at the same time.

"(Signed) Yours, most respectfully,
"*August Belmont and Co.*

"This credit is in favor for *two years from date.*"

The parts of the letter which are printed in Italics, were in manuscript in the original. The rest was the printed form. You will observe that the parts which were in manuscript comprise all those portions of the letter which would require to be varied for different travellers applying for letters, while the printed portion consists of what would be the same for all.

Besides the letter of credit, Grimkie's father recommended to Mrs. Morelle to take a considerable supply of English gold with her—as much as she could conveniently carry—to use when she first landed; for she might desire, he said, to travel about England for a while before going to London, which was the first place where her letter of credit could be made available.

"Besides," said he, "it is a little cheaper for you to carry gold. The gold which you buy here and take with you, does not cost quite so much as that which you obtain there, through your letter of credit; for, besides being repaid for the actual value of the gold, the bankers require something for themselves, as their profit on the transaction."

"That's fair," said Grimkie. "But then why can't we take it *all* in gold, and so get it all cheaper?"

"Because then you lose in interest money more than you save," said his father. "Suppose, for example, a person is going to spend three thousand dollars in a year, in travelling in Europe—fifteen hundred dollars the first six months, and fifteen hundred in the second. Now the last fifteen hundred, if he leaves it at home, well invested, will bring in, during the first half of the year, say forty or fifty dollars, which will much more than pay the banker's commission. So it is better for him to leave it invested, and take it from the banker's when the time comes for using it. And then, besides, the danger of being robbed is very much greater in taking a very large sum in gold with you. It is best, therefore, for you to rely upon your letter of credit, except for what you require at the outset, and that it is well to take with you in gold."

So it was arranged that Grimkie should go with Mrs. Morelle to a money broker's in Wall-street, whose address his father gave him, to get some sovereigns.

A money-broker is a man who keeps the different kinds of money of all the different foreign nations for sale. Merchants, shipmasters, travellers and other persons coming home from foreign parts, are always bringing home certain quantities of this money. As it will not pass current in this country, they usually take it to a money-broker's and sell it. He pays them for it a little less than its intrinsic value. In this way he keeps a supply of all kinds of foreign money constantly on hand, and in passing by his office you often see these coins in the window for sale, just as you see books in the window of a bookstore, or toys in that of a toy-shop, and travellers who wish to visit any foreign countries, or persons who wish to send money there for any purpose, go to these brokers and buy the kind of money which they require—though, of course, they have to pay for it a little *more* than its intrinsic value, just as those who brought it into the country were obliged to sell it for a little less. The difference is the broker's profit.

The coin which Mrs. Morelle wished to buy was sovereigns. The value of the sovereign is a pound. It is divided into twenty shillings, which are represented by silver coins of nearly the size of an American quarter of a dollar.

The sovereign is a gold coin, nearly as large as an American five dollar piece. There is gold enough in a new sovereign fresh from the mint, to come to four dollars and eighty-six cents, as determined by the assaying officers of the United States. The average amount of gold in the sovereigns in circulation is, however, only four dollars and eighty-four cents. That is, the new ones have two cents worth of gold in them more than the average of those in circulation.

How much you have to pay for sovereigns when you go to buy them at a broker's depends upon how many he has in hand, or expects soon to receive, and upon the demand for them. When a great many sovereigns are wanted and the supply is not large, of course the price rises, and in a reverse of circumstances it falls. Grimkie's father told him that probably he would have to pay four ninety, or four ninety-one for them on the day when he went with Mrs. Morelle to purchase them.

If, instead of purchasing sovereigns at the broker's, the traveller obtains them of the banker's through a letter of credit, they cost him, on account of commissions and charges, nearly five dollars apiece. American travellers, therefore, generally reckon the sovereigns which they expend in Europe in their travels, and in the purchases which they make, as so many times five dollars.

On entering the broker's office, Mrs. Morelle and Grimkie at once heard a great chinking of coin, as people were counting it out, either paying or receiving it. There was a long counter on one side of the room, with clerks behind it, and beyond the clerks, against the wall, were shelves, with boxes of coin, and little heaps of coin, some in piles, and some in rolls, enveloped in paper. A man, who looked like a seafaring man, was standing at the counter in one place, with a bag of gold which he had just opened, and he was now pouring out the coin from it. It was a bag of doubloons which he had brought from some Spanish country. Near by was a young man, who was just counting and putting into a bag a quantity of sovereigns which he had been purchasing. There were various others at different places along the counter engaged in similar transactions.

Mrs. Morelle had concluded to reserve about seventy-five dollars, for her expenses in going to Boston, and to invest all the rest of the money which she had with her in sovereigns. But Grimkie, who seemed to want to get hold of as many sovereigns as possible, said to her as they were coming in the carriage toward the office that he thought that seventy-five dollars was more than would be necessary to take them to Boston. But she said that possibly some accident might happen which would lead to extra expense, and it was always best to have enough.

"And then if I have anything left over," said she, "we can purchase sovereigns with it in Boston, the morning before we sail."

Accordingly Grimkie, holding in his hands eight bills of a hundred dollars each, went with Mrs. Morelle to a vacant place at the counter, and said that he wished to buy some sovereigns, and asked the price.

"How many will you want?" asked the clerk.

"About a hundred and sixty," said Grimkie. He had previously made a calculation that he could have rather more than a hundred and sixty for the eight hundred dollars.

"I have got eight hundred dollars here," said Grimkie, "which I wish to change into sovereigns."

"We can let you have them for four ninety," said the clerk.

Then taking a little slip of paper and a pencil he made a calculation, and presently said,

"You can have a hundred and sixty-three sovereigns, and a little over, for the eight hundred dollars."

"How much will one hundred and sixty-five cost?" asked Mrs. Morelle.

The clerk, after figuring a little more on his paper, said that they would come to eight hundred and eight dollars and fifty cents exactly.

"Then let us take a hundred and sixty-five," said Mrs. Morelle, "and I will pay the eight dollars fifty."

So Mrs. Morelle took eight dollars and fifty cents from her purse, and put it with the eight hundred dollars, and Grimkie gave the whole to the clerk. He counted it and put it away, and then proceeded to count out the sovereigns, laying them in piles, as he counted them, of fifty each.

"Would you like a bag to put them in?" asked the clerk.

Grimkie said he would like one very much.

So the clerk gave him a small, brown linen bag, large enough to contain the coin. While Grimkie was putting the money into the bag, it occurred to him that perhaps it would be well to have a little English silver.

"We shall also have need of a little change, Auntie," said he, "when we first land, for the porters or the cabmen."

"I can give you silver for one of the sovereigns," said the clerk, "if you wish."

So Grimkie gave back one of the sovereigns to the clerk, and the clerk in lieu of it counted out twenty silver coins not quite so large as a quarter of a dollar. He left them on the counter for Grimkie to count over after him, and began to attend to another customer.

"That's right, Auntie," said Grimkie: "twenty is right. Twelve pence make a shilling; twenty shillings make a pound."

Grimkie wrapped up the twenty shillings in a

piece of paper, and put them into the mouth of his bag, and then putting the bag in his pocket, he assisted Mrs. Morelle into the carriage, and after getting in himself, he ordered the coachman to drive to the hotel.

CHAPTER V.

THE EMBARKATION.

On Tuesday morning, when Mrs. Morelle and her party arrived at Boston, they learned from an advertisement in the newspaper that they must be on board the next morning at eight o'clock, as the steamer was to sail at nine.

"I am glad of that," said Grimkie; "for now the sooner we are off the better. Only," he added, after a moment's pause, "we shall not have a chance to change the rest of our money."

"True," said Mrs. Morelle; "and I think I shall have nearly forty dollars over, after I have paid the bill at the hotel."

"That would get us eight sovereigns more," said Grimkie.

"I don't know what I shall do with that money," said Mrs. Morelle. "It is in bank bills, which will be of no use in England, and it will make me considerable trouble to carry them with me all the time of my tour."

"Perhaps we might get five-dollar gold pieces with the money here at the hotel," said Grimkie, "and that would be much better than to carry the bills, for we can sell the gold pieces in Liverpool to the brokers there, for nearly as much as they are worth."

"That will be the best thing that we can do," said Mrs. Morelle.

So Grimkie took the money and went to the bar of the hotel, and the barkeeper said he could change it into gold just as well as not. He accordingly gave Grimkie eight half-eagles, and Grimkie, after wrapping them up carefully in a paper by themselves, put them into the top of his money bag, with the rest of the coin, and then put the whole carefully away in his aunt's trunk.

The next morning, at half-past seven, a coach which Grimkie had ordered the night before, came to the private door of the Tremont House, in Tremont Place, and took the whole party in, with their luggage, and conveyed them to East Boston, where the steamer was lying.

As soon as they arrived upon the pier, they found themselves in the midst of a scene of great bustle and excitement.

Carriages were arriving in rapid succession, bringing passengers to the ship. Piles of trunks and carpet-bags were lying upon the pier, and a line of sailorlike-looking men were engaged in taking them on board. As soon as Grimkie's baggage—for from this time he called it all his, since he had now the exclusive charge of it—was set down, Grimkie paid the fare, and the coachman, mounting upon the box, wheeled his carriage round, and drove away. Very soon one of the porters from the ship came and took up one of the trunks to carry it on board.

"Johnnie," said Grimkie, "you go with Aunt and Florence on board, after this man, and see where he puts this trunk, and then come back here. I'll stay in the meantime, and watch the rest."

So John led the way in following the porter over the plank, while his mother and Florence followed *him*. As soon as he got on board, he saw the porter put down the trunk in a sort of open space in the middle of the deck, with a great many others, and in a moment afterward several more were piled up upon it and around it, so that it rapidly disappeared from view.

John found a place near by where Mrs. Morelle could stand, a little out of the way of the crowd, and then immediately hastened back over the plank to where he had left Grimkie on the pier.

"Grimkie," said he, "they have covered our

trunk all up with fifty others, and I don't see how we shall ever get it again."

"Never mind," said Grimkie; "we'll wait and see how the other passengers get theirs."

Just at this moment some porters came and took up the two remaining trunks, and heaving them up upon their shoulders, began to walk with them on board. Grimkie and John followed, bringing with them the valise and several other similar things. When they arrived on board they saw the two trunks deposited with the other baggage, and where they soon began rapidly to disappear from view.

"Now," said Grimkie, "we will go down and put the valise in our state-room."

The deck and all the passages leading below, were crowded with people going and coming. A large proportion of these people were friends of the passengers, who had come to accompany them on board, in order to see the ship and the state-rooms which their friends were to occupy. Grimkie led the way through this crowd, working forward slowly, as well as he could, and followed by the rest of his party. Indeed there were two lines of people moving in contrary directions, and Grimkie supposed that by following the one that was going on, he should sooner or later find his way below.

He was right in this calculation. He was soon conducted to a door which led into a narrow but very elegant passage-way. In the middle of this passage-way was a door to the right, leading into a magnificent saloon, with a walk up and down the middle of it, and rows of long tables on each side. The aspect of this room was very brilliant, but Grimkie had only time to glance at it, for opposite to it, on the other side of the passage-way were three other openings, the center one opening into a most spacious and elegant china closet, and each of the two side ones leading down a flight of winding stairs, with very bright brass hand-rails on the sides to take hold of in descending.

On reaching the foot of the stair-case, the party entered a bewildering mass of passages and open spaces, all elegantly finished, with highly polished woods, and handsomely carpeted, and lighted moreover with strangely placed sky-lights and panes of glass placed in rows near the ceiling. Grimkie thought that he knew from the plan exactly where to look for his aunt's state-room, but he found himself completely bewildered and lost. There were various state-room doors opening all around him. He went into one or two of them and looked at the numbers inscribed upon the berths, but they were not the right ones.

At length he met a very respectable middle aged woman, who seemed to belóng on board. She was in fact the stewardess. Grimkie asked her if she would show him state-room number twenty-three and twenty-four.

"Ah yes," said she, "with a great deal of pleasure. This is it. It is one of the three best state-rooms in the ship."

Grimkie stood back and allowed his aunt to go into the state-room first, and then the other children and finally he himself, followed.

The state-room was in size like what in a house on land would be called a large closet, being about seven feet wide and eight feet long. Across the end of it, and against the side of the ship, were two berths one above another, with pretty curtains before them, and a space underneath the lowermost berth, where trunks might be placed. Along one of the sides there extended a wide settee, covered with a hair-cloth cushion, and on the other side two wash-stands in the two corners, with a short and narrow seat, also covered with a haircloth cushion, between them. There was a looking-glass over the settee, and various little shelves, with ledges upon the outer edge of them, to prevent the things from rolling off in a heavy sea. There were also sundry large brass pins for hanging cloaks and dresses upon, and brass rings projecting from the walls in the corners to put tumblers into.

Opening into the upper berth was a small, round window, deep set in the thickness of the ship's side, and there was also a very thick piece of glass, of prismatic shape, set in the deck above, making a sort of window there, six inches by three. Over the door, too, and extending along the whole of that side of the state-room, was a row of panes of glass, which admitted light from the passage-way, and from other panes set in mysterious recesses above.

Mrs. Morelle as soon as she had entered the state-room, drew back the curtain of the lower berth, and laid her shawl and her parasol upon the bed, while Grimkie placed the valise under the little seat between the two wash-stands.

Mrs. Morelle then sat down upon the settee and looked around to take a survey of the place, and then at the sky-light above. At the same time she drew a long breath and said,

"Ah me! This is rather a small cell to be shut up in as a prisoner for two weeks."

"Oh mother!" exclaimed Florence, "we shall not be shut up here. We can go about all over the ship."

"You children will do that," said Mrs. Morelle, "but I shall be shut up here. I shall be sick."

"But mother you will not be sick all the voyage," said Florence.

"Perhaps not," said she. "I am sure I shall not be very sick, all the voyage. After a day or two I shall be only comfortably sick, and you will all be perfectly well I am quite sure, and can run about wherever you please."

Then rising from her seat she said,

"But I need not begin my imprisonment yet. Let us go up on deck and see the people come on board."

So they all left the state-room, and making their way through the crowd as well as they could, they went up to the upper deck, where they found a great number of ladies and gentlemen assembled in various groups—some standing and others sitting upon settees and camp-stools, while the pier, which was here in full view, was crowded with other parties coming and going, and with porters bringing more trunks and baggage on board.

Grimkie found seats for his party, and they all sat down. They remained in these places an hour, amusing themselves with the extraordinary spectacle which was exhibiting itself around them.

As the time drew nigh for the sailing of the ship, the excitement of the scene was increased by the steam which having now been raised in the boilers to its full tension, and not yet being allowed to expend its energies in turning the paddles, made its escape through the waste-pipe with a thundering roar which made it almost impossible for the friends who were taking leave of each other to hear the parting word. From time to time the bell was rung, loud and rapidly, to warn those who were only on board as visitors to go on shore. A long and crowded procession of these visitors poured over the bridge to the pier, and when all were gone the bridge itself was raised, and hoisted to the shore, by a vast tackle and fall. The noise of the steam now suddenly ceased. The hawsers at the bow and at the stern were cast off, the paddle-wheels commenced their motion, and the ship began slowly to move away from the pier. A moment afterward two guns were fired one after another from the bows of the ship, with a deafening sound. The passengers standing along the hand-railing of the upper deck waved their hats and handkerchiefs to their friends who thronged the pier, and who waved their hats and handkerchiefs in return. Many of them were in tears. Mrs. Morelle herself might have experienced some misgivings and have felt a little homesick and sad, at parting thus from her native land, and setting out upon so long a voyage with only three children, as it were, for her companions,— but she was going to meet her husband; and when a wife is going to meet a husband that she loves, or a mother to her son, she rarely experiences any misgiving. Her heart reposes with so much confidence and hope, upon the end of her journey, that she seldom shrinks very much from any thing to be encountered on the way.

CHAPTER VI.

LIFE ON BOARD SHIP.

THE party enjoyed a very excellent opportunity, as the ship sailed down the harbor, of viewing the scenery of the shores, and of seeing the other ships, steamers and sail-boats, that were going in various directions to and fro. While Mrs. Morelle remained at this seat, Grimkie and John went to take a walk about the ship to see what they could see. There was no difficulty now in going where they pleased, for since the visitors had left the ship and none but the regular passengers remained, there was ample room for all.

Accordingly, Grimkie and John took a long ramble all about the ship. They looked down into the engine-room, and there, at a vast depth below the deck, they saw half-naked stokers shoveling coal into the furnace. They walked along by the ranges of offices which extended on each side of the main deck through the whole middle portion of the ship, like two little streets of shops in a town. . They saw the cow—a monstrous one—shut up in a pen, with the sides of it covered with carpeting and well padded, like the back of a sofa, to prevent the cow from being hurt when thrown against them by the rolling of the ship in a storm. They went into the saloon and were much struck with the brilliancy and magnificence of it. There was one arrangement which particularly attracted their attention. This was a row of hanging shelves extending up and down the room over the tables. These shelves were made of some highly polished wood and were so ornamented with brass mountings that they made quite an elegant appearance. They were all loaded, too, with cut-glass and silver-ware—such as decanters, tumblers, wine-glasses of different colors, castors, and silver spoons,—which added greatly to the brilliance of the effect. The shelves were double, or, as one might say, two stories high, the upper story of each having holes and openings in it of various forms, suited to the various articles which they were to contain. In these openings of the upper board the various vessels were placed, while the bottoms of them rested on the lower board. Each one had thus its own little nest, where it could rest in safety, no matter how much the ship might pitch or roll.

Grimkie found that cards were pinned along

the sides of the table to mark the places where the different passengers were to sit, and there were also in the saloon two or three gentlemen who had cards in their hands, and were looking out for vacant places to put them.

"Ah, yes!" said Grimkie, "we must choose our places at the tables. Father told me about this and I have got the cards in my pocket, all ready. I came very near forgetting it."

So he took out the cards and one of the stewards who was there, helped him to choose good places. After he had pinned the cards to the table-cloth, opposite the seats which they were intended to secure, he and John went up to the upper deck again to where Mrs. Morelle and Florence were sitting. Mrs. Morelle asked John how he liked the ship.

He liked it very well he said. Every thing was complete and secure. The chairs and tables were all screwed down to the floor, and there were nests for all the tumblers, and a sofa for the cow.

The ship was now gradually getting out of the harbor, and coming upon the open sea where she met with a gentle swell over which she rose and fell in a manner very graceful and charming to the eye, but very bewildering and dizzying in its effects upon the brain. Mrs. Morelle and Florence soon went below, where, with the help of Mrs. McGregor, the stewardess, who was extremely kind and attentive to them, they undressed themselves and went to bed. Mrs. Morelle got into the lower berth, but as Florence felt a little afraid to climb up into the upper one, Mrs. McGregor made a bed for her upon the settee, where she could lie very comfortably.

Grimkie and John remained up and about the decks all that day. At times they felt sick and uncomfortable, but they were so much excited by the new and strange scenes which continually attracted their attention that they were extremely unwilling to go to their state-room. From time to time they paid Mrs. Morelle and Florence a visit, but they found them lying silent and motionless, and very little inclined to talk. At twelve o'clock there was a grand luncheon in the dining saloon, with nearly all the passengers at the tables. At four a still grander dinner, though the places of the ladies were generally vacant.

The ship's bells tolled the hours regularly through the afternoon and evening watches, and at eight o'clock both Grimkie and John were very ready to go to bed. Grimkie allowed John to have the lower berth because it was so much easier to get into. There was no real difficulty however in respect to the upper berth, for Mrs.

McGregor, when the boys were ready to go to bed, brought in a very nice step-ladder with iron hooks at the upper end of it to hook into the edge of the berth. She hooked the ladder on the berth and planted the lower end of it upon the floor, and then went away, saying that the ladder could remain there all night.

"It is a very nice ladder," said John, "and it must be easy going up. But I never saw a ladder with hooks in it before. A ladder will stand steady enough without hooks."

"On *land* it would," said Grimkie. "But at sea, when the ship is rolling heavily in a gale of wind, the ladder must have claws to hold on by."

"I hope we shall have a good gale of wind," said John, after a brief pause. "I want to see if I can go up that ladder in it."

John was however evidently not much inclined to talk. He undressed himself in silence and crept into his berth. Grimkie also mounted the ladder and climbed over from the top of it into his. After covering himself up with the bed clothes and getting as well settled as was possible in so hard and narrow a bed, he extended his head over the edge of his berth so as to look down toward John's berth below, and said,

"Johnnie, are you comfortable?"

"Yes," said John.

"Are you sleepy?" said Grimkie.

"No," said John, "but I am sick."

"Never mind," said Grimkie. "Say your prayers to yourself, and then shut up your eyes and go to sleep, and forget all about it."

For several days after this time the condition of our party of travelers was quite forlorn. Grimkie himself, in fulfillment of a positive resolution which he had made, clambered down from his berth, and went up to the saloon to all his meals, though frequently without being able to eat any thing when he got there. On these occasions he always went into Mrs. Morelle's stateroom, to see how his aunt and Florence were. He found them generally lying in their beds, Mrs. Morelle in the berth, and Florence upon the settee, silent and motionless, and not at all inclined to conversation. His aunt opened her eyes and smiled faintly when he came in and usually asked him some questions about the progress of the ship. The weather was cold, rainy and foggy, and although the air was in itself tolerably calm, the motion of the ship through the water produced a raw and chilly wind across the decks, which made it impossible to remain there long without extreme discomfort.

On the second night out, about eight o'clock, the engine stopped. Grimkie, who was always ready at a moment's notice to go into his aunt's stateroom whenever she knocked upon the partition to call him, or there was any other occasion for going in to see her, and who for this purpose undressed very little during all the first part of the voyage, immediately climbed down from his berth, and slipping on a great coat which he kept always at hand, in lieu of a dressing gown, he opened his aunt's door.

The moment that he opened it, Mrs. Morelle raised her head suddenly, and asked him in a tone of alarm, what was the matter.

"I don't think any thing at all is the matter, Auntie," said he. "They are always stopping the engine on these voyages—to tighten up a screw or something or other."

"But Grimkie," said she, "I wish you would go and see if you can not find out what is the matter. I am afraid that something has happened."

There was, indeed, something almost awful in the solemn stillness which reigned throughout the ship, now that the engine had ceased its motion, and the ship lay rocking upon the waves as if powerless and helpless. Grimkie immediately left the stateroom in order to go upon deck, and Mrs. Morelle's alarm was very much increased a moment after he had gone, by a burst of steam from the steam-pipe, which suddenly began to be heard, occasioned by the letting off of the surplus steam, which, as it could now no longer be employed in driving the paddle-wheels, it was necessary to allow to escape into the atmosphere.

A moment after this sound began to be heard however, Mrs. McGregor came into the cabin, to say to Mrs. Morelle, that she must not be alarmed at the stopping of the engine, for there was nothing the matter.

"They have only stopped to sound," said she. "You see we are drawing nigh to Halifax, and it is very thick and dark, and they can not see the land. So they have to sound and go on cautiously. We shall go on again presently."

So saying Mrs. McGregor went away in order to convey the same relief and reassurance to the ladies in the other staterooms.

Grimkie went up on deck, but he could see nothing. The night was dark, and a heavy mist mingled with rain, was driving along the decks. He could hear the voices of some of the sailors occasionally, talking in ordinary tones, in the forward part of the vessel, and now and then a command given by an officer, but otherwise all was still.

Grimkie returned to the stateroom, and there found how much his aunt had been relieved by having learned that they had stopped the ship to sound.

"I was sure there could not be anything the matter," said Grimkie. "So you must shut your eyes, Auntie, and go to sleep, and not pay any attention after this to any thing you hear. There are ever so many things going on in such a ship, and when any thing unusual happens we must not mind it. Whenever there is any danger—or at least whenever there is any thing for us to do, Mrs. McGregor will be sure to come and tell us."

"That is true," said Mrs. Morelle, "and I will try not to be afraid again."

"But if you *should be* afraid at any time, Auntie," continued Grimkie," just knock at the head of your berth and I shall hear."

So saying Grimkie bade his aunt good night and went back to his stateroom. As for John he heard nothing of all this, having slept soundly through the whole.

The steamer was soon put in motion again, but in the course of an hour she stopped anew. Grimkie was asleep, but the stopping wakened him. He knew it was not midnight by the stateroom light which was still burning. There was a little three-cornered box partitioned off in a corner between the two staterooms, with a door opening into the passage-way, and ground glass sides toward the staterooms. Into this box a lighted candle was placed by a steward standing in the passage-way, every evening, as soon as it was dark, and this gave a dim and indistinct light in the two staterooms adjoining it, through the ground glass panes. This was all the light for the staterooms that was allowed.

Moreover, as this light was put out at midnight, it afforded the passengers the means of knowing, when they awoke in the night, whether it was before or after midnight, by observing whether their light had gone out or was still burning.

Grimkie was awakened from his sleep by the stopping of the engine the second time, and he remained awake long enough to observe that his light was still burning. He, however, soon fell asleep again.

He awoke after this several times during the night and found the ship sometimes at rest, and sometimes in motion. On one of these occasions he heard a great sound of trampling upon the deck, as of persons going to and fro, and a sort of thumping, such as would be occasioned by the moving heavy boxes about upon deck. He determined to go up and see what was the matter.

So he climbed down from his berth, put on his

great coat, his overshoes, and his cap, and went up to the deck. He saw lights, and the dim forms of many men were going to and fro forward and on the side of the ship a long range of black masses which looked so strange that they quite bewildered him. The wind blew, and the mist and rain were driven into his face so as almost to blind him. As he stood at the head of the stairs looking out, a passenger came by to go in.

"What is it?" asked Grimkie.

"Halifax," said the passenger. "I'm thankful that we have got in at last. We lost five hours beating about outside in the fog before we could get in."

Grimkie was determined to see Halifax, so he went out upon the main deck and thence along to the foot of a narrow winding stair which led up to the upper deck, and thence forward to the great funnel where he thought he could find a little shelter. He saw some lights glancing about upon the pier, and the dark and indistinct forms of men moving to and fro, and a range of black spectral looking roofs extending along the shore. But it was so cold, and the mist and rain were driven so furiously into his face by the wind, that he was glad to go below, saying to himself as he went,

"We may have better luck perhaps when we

come back, and get to Halifax in the day time."

When he awoke the next time he knew by the jar, and by the rocking motion of the ship, that they were not only on their way again, but were once more out upon the open sea.

Everything went on much in this way for a day or two longer. It was cold and wet upon the decks, and dreary and silent below. The horizon in every direction was obscured by fogs and mists, and the decks were kept always wet by driving rains which were continually sweeping over the sea. Grimkie went up regularly to his meals, but he was glad to come back again as soon as possible to his berth, and the rest of the party kept their berths all the time. Mrs. McGregor brought them soup, and porridge, and tea and toast, and other things, at regular intervals, but often they were taken away again, scarcely touched, and during the intervals of these visits Mrs. Morelle and Florence remained in their berths, sometimes hour after hour without speaking a word.

The only amusement which they had was to listen for the sound of the ship's bells as they tolled the slow progress of the hours, and to hear the news which Grimkie brought in to them from time to time, in respect to the progress of the voyage.

During a great portion of this time Mrs. Morelle was kept in a constant state of uneasiness, by the blowing of a monstrous steam trumpet which was attached to the engine, and which was sounded every two or three minutes, when the fog was too thick ahead to allow them to see whether any vessels were in the way. The intention in blowing this trumpet is, that if there should be any such vessels in the line of the steamer's advance, they may hear the sound and blow horns or fire guns in response, and then the steamer might be turned to one side to avoid them.

This blowing of the steam trumpet in a fog, is an example of the extreme caution and care which marks the whole management of the Cunard steamers, and which inspires the public with so great a degree of confidence in them. Many steamers in such cases push boldly on, without making any signals, trusting to the chance of not meeting anything by the way. I once heard the captain of a steamer say, when we were going on through a dense fog, on the Atlantic, without taking any of these precautions, that there was about as little chance of a steamer's coming into collision with another vessel when pursuing her way upon the ocean, as there would be of hitting a bird by firing a gun at random into the air.

There is, however, something rather trying to the nerves of timid lady passengers, in hearing the unearthly scream of this awful trumpet sound its note of alarm, at regular intervals at midnight, while they lie sick, miserable and helpless in their berths. When for a time the sound ceases, indicating that the horizon has become so cleared ahead that the lookout-men can see, their hearts revive within them, only to sink again however when a few minutes later perhaps, or perhaps a few hours, the frightful sound is heard again, sending its screaming note of alarm far and wide over the sea.

In a day or two after leaving Halifax, the ship came upon the banks of Newfoundland, a vast area of foggy and stormy sea, the darkest, dreariest and most dangerous portion of the Atlantic. Indeed upon these banks almost all conceivable dangers of the sea seem to congregate. The water is shallow upon the banks and that brings fish, and the fish bring fishermen in immense numbers, and the steamers in dark and foggy nights and days are in constant danger of running foul of them. The gulf stream brings a vast quantity of comparatively warm water here from the Gulf of Mexico and the tropics, while at the same time the winds and currents from Baffin's bay float down immense fields and mountains of ice, which chill the air and produce fogs, mists, rains and driving storms.

The steamer was two or three days in crossing the banks, and during almost all this time she was enveloped in thick misty rains, which kept the decks continually wet, and covered the surface of the sea in every direction, concealing the fishing vessels, and the icebergs, and all other dangers entirely from view. The trumpet was kept continually blowing, by which means it was probable that fishermen might be warned,—but the greatest danger was from icebergs, for which, of course, no warning could be of any avail.

At length, on Monday evening, Mrs. McGregor comforted all the ladies, by saying, that the next morning the ship would be off the banks, and that then in all probability they would find good weather. This proved to be the case. Grimkie went up to the deck before breakfast, and he found instead of thick mists and rain covering the whole surface of the water, only a stratum of clouds in the sky, while the horizon was open and clear in every direction around. Mrs. Morelle and Florence too, had now become somewhat accustomed to the motion of the ship, and their appetites began to return. And when at length, about the middle of the forenoon, a sunbeam made its appearance in the little prismatic piece of glass which was set in the ceiling of the stateroom, overhead, they began to feel quite cheerful and happy. The same effect was produced in many other staterooms, occupied by ladies. They began to feel as if they could get up and dress themselves, so as to eat their dinners in a somewhat civilized manner.

Things improved after this every day. The ladies of the different staterooms began to become somewhat acquainted with each other through Mrs. McGregor, who informed them of each other's condition, and conveyed messages of politeness and good will to and fro. There were a number of children too, who played in the passages, and thus became acquainted with each other, and were brought in by each other to visit their mothers still lying perhaps upon their settees or in their berths.

Mrs. Morelle became so well acquainted with one of her neighbors who occupied the stateroom opposite to hers, across the passage-way, one which was quite small and confined, that she often invited her to come and dine with her. Sometimes Florence was of the party too, but generally from this time Florence preferred to go up to the great saloon, and take dinner there with Grimkie and John. In such cases she would come after leaving the table and look in at her mother's stateroom, where she usually found her mother and her visitor enjoying themselves very well indeed, with nice beef-steaks, fried potatoes, and tumblers of iced lemonade.

After this time every thing went on smoothly and prosperously till the end of the voyage. After leaving the banks there are no special dangers to be apprehended by a Cunard ship, in crossing the Atlantic, and every body on board was now in good spirits, looking forward with great pleasure to the approaching termination of the voyage.

At length, on Saturday afternoon, about four o'clock, news came down to the ladies in the staterooms that land was in sight. The land first seen consisted of certain high mountains in the vicinity of the town of Killarney, in the southwestern part of Ireland. A few hours later the ship passed Cape Clear, which is the southernmost point of Ireland, and then bearing a little to the northward followed the coast toward the Cove of Cork, where she was to touch in order to land passengers and mails.

She reached this place between eight and nine o'clock. A tender came off from Queenstown, which is a town situated at the mouth of the harbor, to take the mails and the passengers that were to be landed here. The other passengers, who were to go on with the ship to Liverpool, and who were now all in excellent spirits as they considered their voyage substantially over, established themselves upon camp-stools and settees upon the upper deck, watching the operation of putting the mails on board the tender, or looking upon the green shores of Ireland, which as the sun had but just gone down, were brightly illuminated by the golden radiance of the western sky.

The passengers all seemed to feel a peculiar pleasure in thus approaching the land again; and they watched the shores, until, as it grew dark, one after another they went below for the night. Grimkie and John remained some time after Mrs. Morell and Florence had retired.

The next day being Sunday, divine service was held in the saloon, and though the ship was out of sight of land for a large part of the day, the ladies were nearly all well enough, not only to attend service in the saloon, but also to sit upon the upper deck nearly all the afternoon, to watch for the reappearance of the land, and to talk about what they were to do after their arrival. As for Mrs. Morelle she had concluded to postpone forming any definite plan in respect to her tour, until she was safe on shore.

The children, who had become acquainted on the voyage, finding they were so soon to bid good-by to their new friends, made various projects of excursions together, in case they should meet each other in the course of their travels.

CHAPTER VI.

MORNING IN LIVERPOOL.

Most heartily glad were Mrs. Morelle and Florence to set foot once more upon dry land. Grimkie and John, though on the whole well pleased to arrive at the end of the voyage, had, nevertheless, found so much to amuse them, and to occupy their minds, on board the ship, especially during the last few days, that they had not been at all impatient to reach the shore. Immediately on landing they all got into a cab and drove to the Waterloo Hotel, where rooms had been ordered for them beforehand by Mr. Jay, who had written to Liverpool for that purpose, the week before the *Europa* sailed.

They found the rooms all ready for them,—a parlor and two bed-rooms. The parlor was on the front of the house, and looked out upon the street. The bed-rooms were in the rear. One of the bed-rooms was for Mrs. Morelle and Florence, and the other for Grimkie and John.

Of course they all went to bed early. They found it inexpressibly delightful to have a good wide and soft bed to get into, and to go to sleep without being rocked, though Mrs. Morelle and Florence still continued to feel the rocking motion of the ship whenever they shut their eyes.

In an English hotel the usages are entirely different from those which prevail in America. There are no stated hours for meals, and no public room except one for gentlemen. In an American hotel there is no objection to a little bustle and life. Indeed one of the charms of traveling in America is the pleasure of witnessing the bustle and life of the hotels. In England, on the other hand, the hotels are kept as still and quiet as possible. The idea is, especially when a lady arrives at one, to make it as much as possible like her own private house. Often the landlord, the landlady, the porter, the waiter and the chambermaid, meet her at the door when she comes, and receive her just as if they were her own private servants, and the house was her own private house. The porter receives and takes care of the baggage, the landlady conducts the guests to their parlor, and from the parlor the chambermaid presently shows the way to her chambers. The lady establishes herself in these rooms just as if she were at home. She has all her meals with her own party, in her own room, ordering just what she likes, and fixing the hours to suit her own convenience. The fact that there may be other parties in the hotel, living in the same way, is kept as much as possible out of view. Thus it happens that a lady is sometimes several days at a hotel, and one of her best friends is there too all the time, living in another wing or in rooms approached by some other passage-way, while she knows nothing about it.

Of course there was a great deal to be done that evening before the members of our party were ready to go to bed, but when finally bedtime arrived, Mrs. Morelle said that she should not wish to have breakfast very early the next morning, but the children might get up, she added, as early as they pleased, and if they wished, go out and take a walk.

"Only, you must be back by a quarter to nine," said she, "for I intend to have breakfast at nine. And Florence," she added, "if you are up in time, I should like to have you order it."

"How shall I order it, mother?" asked Florence.

"When you go out into the parlor you will find the table already set. The waiters always set all the tables in the different parlors early in the morning, when they arrange the rooms.

You must then ring the bell and the waiter will come. Tell him that your mother will have breakfast at nine o'clock, and also tell him what you will have."

"And what shall we have mother?" asked Florence.

"You may have whatever you please," said Mrs. Morelle, "only I should like a fried sole for one thing."

The sole is a remarkably fine fish, in some sense peculiar to England. It is particularly nice when fried, and the Americans generally count a great deal upon having one for breakfast on the morning after they arrive in Liverpool from a voyage across the Atlantic.

Liverpool lies so far to the north, that the sun, in the middle of June, rises very early,—between three and four o'clock—and it is quite light at half past two. Grimkie was deceived by this very early dawn, and he got up about three o'clock on the following morning, and began to dress himself, but happening to look at his watch he saw how early it was, and so he went to bed again.

When he next awoke, it was half past six. So he determined to get up. John got up too. They both dressed themselves and went out into the parlor, but they found that the shutters were not open.

"John," said Grimkie, "the waiters are all asleep. We will go out and take a walk and come back again by and by."

So the two boys passed down stairs and went out into the streets. There were milk carts and other such things going about, but the shops were all shut, and there were no signs of opening them.

"John," said Grimkie, "the shopmen are all asleep too, and there is nothing to see here—but let us go down to the landing. We shall find somebody awake there you may depend."

Now there is something very curious at Liverpool in respect to the arrangements made for the shipping, something that is especially well calculated to interest such boys as Grimkie and John, and that is the system of docks and landings. The tide rises and falls so much that the ordinary system of fixed piers for vessels to lie at, and rise and fall with the tide, will not answer. Accordingly there have been built a range of immense docks, extending along the shore for many miles. The ships go into these docks through vast gates which are opened at high tide, when of course the river and the docks are both full. Then the gates are shut to keep the water in, and thus although the tide in the river may go down very low, the ships within the docks, are kept afloat all the time—the water there being kept up by the resistance of the gates, which are made of immense size and strength, in order to enable them to sustain the pressure.

Thus in sailing up the river opposite to Liverpool the voyager sees nothing for miles along the shore but a lofty wall, of prodigious size interrupted here and there by towers, gateways, and other curious structures—and beyond it a forest of masts and steamboat funnels, rising above it, in countless thousands. The wall is the outer line of the docks, and the masts and funnels seen beyond belong to the ships and steamers which are lying within.

Grimkie and John went down to the shore and rambled about for an hour or more among these docks. They saw immense numbers of ships floating in the basins—which were full of water, although it was low tide in the river outside—and the draw-bridge and gates connecting one lock with another, and vessels loading and unloading, and men hoisting boilers and machinery into steamers by means of prodigious iron cranes, and other such spectacles.

They also saw the landing-stage, which is one of the wonders of Liverpool. It is an immense floating wharf which rises and falls with the tide so as always to preserve the same level in respect to the water. Here all the ferry boats, and tug boats, and tenders, and other small steamers land, as well as row boats and sail boats innumerable, the coming and going of which make the great landing-stage one of the busiest places in the world.

The boys were so much interested in what they saw, that instead of getting back to the hotel at eight o'clock as they had intended, it was a quarter of nine when they arrived. They found that Florence had ordered breakfast, and that the table was set. There was also a pleasant little coal fire burning in the grate, for the morning was cool. In a short time Mrs. Morelle appeared, and soon afterward the whole party sat down to breakfast.

CHAPTER VIII.

PLANS FORMED.

"Now children," said Mrs. Morelle, while she and the children were at breakfast, "since we are safe on shore, we can begin to talk about our plans. It is now about the middle of June. Mr. Morelle will not arrive in London until September. So that we have two months and a half to spend in rambling about. And the question is where we shall go."

"*You* must decide that mother," said Florence.

"Yes," replied Mrs. Morelle, "I will decide it, but first I wish to hear what you all have to say about it. You may all propose the plans which you would prefer, and then I will take the subject into consideration and decide."

The children then all began to talk about the different tours which they had heard the passengers speak of on board the ship, toward the end of the voyage, when they had become well enough to take out their maps and guide-books, and to consult together about the tours which they were to make. Florence said that there was a beautiful region called the lake country, full of mountains and lakes, which lay to the north of Liverpool, in the counties of Cumberland and Westmoreland. The Isle of Wight was proposed too, which is a very charming island lying off the southern coast of England, and a great place of resort for parties travelling for health or pleasure.

John said that for his part he would like to go directly to Paris. His motive for this was partly the long and rapid journey by railway and steamboat which it would require, but chiefly because he wished to see the performances at the Hippodrome, a famous place in Paris for equestrian shows, of which he had heard very glowing accounts before he left America.

When it came to Grimkie's turn to propose a plan, he said that what he should like best, if he thought that his aunt and Florence would like it, would be to go to the Orkney Islands.

"To the Orkney Islands!" exclaimed Mrs. Morelle in a tone of surprise; "why they are beyond the very northern extremity of Scotland."

"Yes, Auntie, I know they are," said Grimkie; "that is the reason why I want to go and see them."

Mrs. Morelle paused a moment, and seemed to be thinking.

"Florence," said she, at length, "go into our bedroom and get my little atlas. You will find it on the table there. I took it out of the trunk this morning."

Mrs. Morelle always carried a small atlas with her, especially when travelling with the children, for she found that occasions were continually arising in which it was necessary, or at least very desirable, to refer to the map.

Florence went out, and in a few minutes returned bringing the atlas with her.

Mrs. Morelle took the atlas and opened it at the map of Scotland. After examining the map attentively, she turned to the map of North America.

"The Orkney Islands extend as far up as latitude fifty-nine and a half," said she, "and the lower point of Greenland is only sixty. So that you would take us to within half a degree of the latitude of Greenland."

"Yes, Auntie," said Grimkie, "that is just it. To think that we can go so far north as that and have good roads and good comfortable inns all the way."

"But we should have to go a part of the way by sea," said Mrs. Morelle. "The Orkneys are islands at some distance from the main land."

"Only six miles, Auntie," said Grimkie. "It is only across the Pentland Firth, and that is only six miles wide."

"But are not the seas in that region very stormy?"

"Yes, Auntie," said Grimkie, "they are the stormiest seas in the world. Those are the seas that the old Norsemen used to navigate, between the coasts of Norway and Scotland, and the Orkney and Shetland Islands and Iceland. The Norsemen were the greatest sailors in the world. They lived almost always on the water, and the harder it blew the better they liked it. I want to go and see where they used to sail."

Grimkie had recently been studying history at the Chateau, and it was there that he had learned about the wonderful exploits which those old sea kings, as they were sometimes called, used to perform in the ships in which they navigated these stormy northern seas. They were very rude and violent men, and they seemed to consider that they had a right to everything that they could find, no matter where, provided they were strong enough to take it. The richest or the most daring among them, who found means to build or buy one or more vessels, would enlist a party of followers, and with this horde make descents upon any of the coasts in all those regions, and plunder the people of their cattle, or seize their little town. Sometimes they would take possession of certain places on the coast and make agreements with the people living there, that if they would give them a certain portion of their cattle every year, they would protect them from any other marauders who might come to rob them. This the people would consent to do, and thus the foundation was laid for territorial governments, on the different coasts adjoining these northern seas.

In process of time the Norsemen and their descendants extended their incursions not only to the islands north of Scotland and to Scotland itself, but also to the coasts of England and Ireland, and at last even of France, where they settled a country, which, from their occupancy of it, received the name of Normandy, which name it retains to the present day.

It was among these rude men, and in these boisterous and terrible seas, where a dismal twilight reigns almost supreme for half the year, and winds and fogs and ice, and sweeping and impetuous tides, have almost continual possession of the sea, that the progenitors of the present race of British and American seamen had their origin. The case is often referred to in history, as affording a conspicuous illustration of the effect which the encountering of difficulty and danger produces, in stimulating the exertions of men, and developing the highest capacities of their nature.

"There is another reason," said Grimkie, "why I should like to go *now* to the Orkney Islands, and that is because it is so near the summer solstice. I have a great desire to get as far north as I can in the time of the summer solstice. Even here the sun rises now between three and four, and it is quite light at two. In the Orkneys there can scarcely be any night at all."

Grimkie it seems had been studying astronomy as well as history, at the Chateau, and so he was quite learned about the summer solstice and other such things. It may be well, however, for me to explain, for the sake of the younger portion of my readers, that the phrase summer solstice refers, for the northern hemisphere, to that portion of the year, when the sun, in his apparent motion, comes farthest to the north, as the winter solstice relates to that portion of the year when the sun declines farthest to the south.

The summer solstice occurs on the twenty-first or twenty-second of June, and the winter solstice on the twenty-first or twenty-second of December.

In the summer solstice the days are longest and the nights shortest. In the winter solstice the days are shortest and the nights longest— that is, to all people living in northern latitudes.

Now it is a very curious circumstance, the cause of which it would be somewhat difficult to explain without showing it by means of a globe, that the difference in length between the days and the nights increases greatly the farther north we go. On or near the equator the difference is very little, at any part of the year. The days throughout the whole year are very nearly twelve hours long, and the nights too. At the pole, however, if it were possible for any one to reach the pole, the day would continue during the whole twenty-four hours for six months in the year, and then the night would continue through the whole twenty-four hours during the remaining six months. In the latitude of the southern part of Greenland, the days, at the time of the summer solstice, are more than eighteen hours long, and the nights not quite six.

There is another remarkable phenomenon too, to be observed in high northern latitudes, in the time of the summer solstice, which Grimkie was very desirous of verifying by his own observation, and that is the long continuance of the twilight, and the very early appearance of the dawn. The reason of this is that the path of the sun is so oblique to the horizon, or in other words the sun goes down in so slanting a direction, that it is a long time after sunset before he gets low enough to withdraw his light entirely from view.

"I should think," said Grimkie, "that in the Orkney Islands it would be light nearly all night. The sun does not set there now till after nine o'clock, and it rises again before three, and so I should think the twilight would not be over before the dawn would begin. And I want to go and see if it really is so."

"It would be very curious indeed," said Florence, "to have it light all night, and no moon. I should like to see it myself, if it really is so.

"But then," she added, after a pause, "we should have to sit up all night to see it."

"No," said Grimkie. "We might get up from time to time, and look out the window. Or perhaps we might be travelling all night somewhere, and then we should see it."

After some farther conversation, Mrs. Morelle said that she would not decide at once in respect to Grimkie's plan, but would wait until she had obtained some farther information.

"Or rather," she said, "until *you* have obtained some farther information for me. After breakfast you may go to a bookstore and buy a good travelling map of Scotland, and also a railway guide. Florence and John may go with you, if they please. Then some time during the day you may study out the different ways of going, and see which you think is the best way. You must find out where the steamer sails from too, to take us across the six miles of water. Then at dinner to-day you can tell me what you have found out, and show me by the map, exactly which way we shall have to go, and what sort of conveyances we shall have for the different portions of the journey. Then when I have all the facts before me I can decide."

Grimkie accordingly bought the map and the guide book, and he spent more than two hours that day in studying them so as to make himself as thoroughly acquainted as possible with every thing pertaining to the route. Mrs. Morelle did not assist him in these researches. In fact she was out shopping during most of the time while Grimkie was making them. Besides she thought it best to leave him to investigate the case as well as he could himself, in the first instance, without any aid.

Accordingly, when the party were assembled for dinner that day, and just before the waiter brought the dinner in, Mrs. Morelle asked Grimkie what sort of report he had to make about the way of reaching the Orkney Islands.

"I have some bad news for you, in the first place," said Grimkie. "We shall have a great deal more than six miles to go in a steamer."

"How is that?" asked Mrs. Morelle.

"Because there is no steamer that goes across in the shortest place," said Grimkie. "There is a sail boat that goes that way, to take the mails, but we could not go in the sail boat very well. The only large steamer is one that goes from Edinburgh. The only places where it stops are Aberdeen and Wick. Wick is the last place it touches at. And from Wick to Kirkwall, which is the town where we land in the Orkneys, it is about sixty miles. So that we should have a steamer voyage of five or six hours to take."

"That is bad news indeed," said Mrs. Morelle.

"But then there is one thing favorable about it," continued Grimkie, "and that is that there is only six miles of the voyage that is in an open sea. We should be sheltered by the land on one side all the way, excepting for about six miles We might at any rate go as far as Wick, and then see how the weather is. If the sea is smooth and calm, then we might go on board the steamer. If not we might wait for the next steamer or give

it up altogether. All the way from here to Wick there will be no difficulty. It will be a very pleasant journey."

Grimkie then unfolded his map in order to explain to his aunt the general features of the country so far as they affected the different modes of travelling to the north of Scotland.

"Here is Wick," said Grimkie, pointing to the situation of that town on the northwest coast of Scotland. It lies as the reader will see by the map, north of a great bay formed by the union of Murray and Dornock Firths. Grimkie pointed out the situation of Wick and also that of Inverness, which lies in the bottom of the bay, at the head of Murray Firth.

"The steamer," he says, "sails from Edinburgh once a week. She touches at Aberdeen, for that is directly in her way, on the eastern coast."

Here Grimkie pointed out the situation of Aberdeen.

"But she does not go to Inverness," continued Grimkie, "although that is a very large and important town, because that would take her too much out of her way. So she steers right across the mouth of the bay, where she must be in the open sea for some time, and makes for Wick. There she takes in freight and passengers, and then sails again north along the coast to the Orkney Islands. The town where she stops in the Orkneys is Kirkwall. After that she sails on and goes to the Shetland Islands, fifty or sixty miles farther over the open sea."

"But Grimkie," said Mrs. Morelle, "why did not you propose to go to the Shetland Islands instead of the Orkneys, while you were about it? You would be still more among the Norsemen's seas there, and the nights would be still shorter."

"Ah!" said Grimkie, "that was my discretion, Auntie. I should like very much to go on to the end of the route, and to see the Shetland ponies, but I knew that you and Florence would not like so long a voyage, and so I only proposed going to the Orkneys."

"That *was* discretion indeed," said Mrs. Morelle. "But tell us the rest of the plan. How about getting to Wick?"

"The next stage this side of Wick," said Grimkie, "is Inverness. From Inverness to Wick we should go by stage-coach. That we should all like. You said the other day, on board ship, that you would like one more good ride in an English stage-coach, and here is an excellent chance. The road winds in and out to pass round the locks and firths, and then coasts along the sea delightfully. At least so my guide book says. There is one splendid pass which it goes through, equal to Switzerland."

"I should like that very much," said Mrs. Morelle. "And now how about getting to Inverness?"

"There are three ways," said Grimkie. "We can go by the railroads on the eastern side of the island, or by coaches and posting up through the center, or by inland steam navigation on the western side."

Grimkie then went on to explain what he had learned by long study of the maps and guide books during the day. The information which he communicated was substantially as follows:

The western part of Scotland north of Glasgow is so mountainous, and so intersected in every direction with long and narrow bays setting in from the sea, and also with inland lakes, that no railroad can well be made there. By connecting these lakes, however, and by cutting across one or two narrow necks of land, and making canals and locks along the sides of some rapid rivers, a channel of inland navigation has been opened, by which steamers can pass all the way from Glasgow to Inverness, through the very heart of the country. The route of the steamers in taking this voyage, for some portion of the way, lies along the shore of the sea, but it is in places where the water is so sheltered by islands and by lofty promontories and headlands, that the ocean swell has very little access to it in any part of the way.

On the eastern coast, on the other hand, the country is comparatively smooth and well cultivated, and a line of railroad extends on this side all the way from Edinburgh to Inverness. Thus the party might, as Grimkie explained the case to them, either go, up to Inverness from Edinburgh by railroad, on the eastern side, through a smooth and beautiful country filled with green and fruitful fields, and with thriving villages and towns,—or by steamboat from Glasgow on the western side, among dark mountains and frowning precipices, and wild but beautiful solitudes. Florence voted at once and very eagerly in favor of the mountains.

"Then there is a third course still that we can take," said Grimkie; "we can go up through the center of the island."

"And how shall we travel in that case?" asked Mrs. Morelle.

"There is no railroad yet through the center," said Grimkie, "and no steamboat route. So we should have to go by coach, or else by a hired carriage."

"And what sort of a country is it?" asked Florence.

"Some parts of it are very beautiful," said Grimkie, "and some parts are very wild. We should go through the estates of some of the grandest noblemen in Great Britain. The guide book says that one duke that lives there planted about twenty-five millions of trees on his grounds, but I don't believe it."

"It *may* be so," said Mrs. Morelle.

"Twenty-five millions is a great many," said Grimkie.

"I don't see where he could get so many trees," said John.

"Probably he raised them from seed in his own nurseries," said Mrs. Morelle.

"He could not have nurseries big enough to raise so many," said John.

"Let us see," said Grimkie. "Suppose he had a nursery a mile square and the little trees grew in it a foot apart. We will call a mile five thousand feet. It is really more than five thousand feet, but we will call it that for easy reckoning. That would give us five thousand rows and five thousand trees in a row—five thousand times five thousand."

Grimkie took out his pencil and figured with it

for a moment, on the margin of a newspaper, and then said,

"It makes exactly twenty-five millions. So that if he had a nursery a mile square, and planted the trees a foot apart, he would have just enough."

"Never mind the Duke of Athol's trees," said Mrs. Morelle. "Let us finish planning our journey."

But here the door opened and two waiters came in bringing the dinner. So the whole party took their seats at the table. Afterward, while they were sitting at the table, Mrs. Morelle asked Grimkie what he had concluded upon as the best way for them to take of all the three which he had described, in case they should decide to go to the Orkney Islands.

"You see, Auntie," said he, "we shall of course go by railway from here to Glasgow, and it will make a pleasant change to take the steamboat there. It is a beautiful steamboat and excellently well managed. It is used almost altogether for pleasure travelling, and every thing is as nice in it as a pin. Then it must be very curious to see the green glens and the sheep pastures, and the highland shepherds on the mountains, as we are sailing along. Then when we get to Inverness we shall change again into the stage-coach, to go to

Wick, and at Wick we shall take the deep sea steamer. So we shall have a series of pleasant changes all the way."

"I am not sure how pleasant the last one will be," said Mrs. Morelle.

"If we have pleasant weather and a smooth sea, I think it will be very pleasant indeed," said Grimkie. "It will be amusing to think how far we are going away, and also to see what kind of people there will be going to the Orkney and Shetland Islands."

"But suppose it should not be pleasant weather and a smooth sea."

"Then we will not go," said Grimkie. "We will stop at Wick and come back again, if we do not wish to wait for the next steamer. It will be a very curious and interesting journey to Wick, even if we do not go any farther at all."

Mrs. Morelle said that she would consider the subject, and give her decision the next morning.

The next morning she told the children that she had concluded to go, and to follow the plan which Grimkie had marked out for the journey.

"But there is one thing that we must not overlook," said she. "We must be sure that we have got money enough. So you must make a calculation how long it will take us to go, and how much it will cost. Of course you can not calculate exactly, but you can come near enough for our purpose. When you have made the calculation, put down the items on paper and show it to me."

Grimkie made the calculation as his aunt had requested. He did not attempt to estimate the expense of each day precisely. That would have been impossible. He reckoned in general the hotel expenses, all the way, at so much a day, from the number of days which it would require, and then from the railway guide and other books he found what the fares would be for the travelling part of the work. He also made a liberal allowance for porterage, coach hire, and other such things. When he had made out his account he gave it to Mrs. Morelle, and she showed it to the keeper of the hotel, and asked him if he thought that was a just estimate. Mr. Lynn, after examining it carefully, said that he thought it was a very good estimate indeed, and that the allowances were all liberal ; and as the total came entirely within the amount which Mrs. Morelle had with her in sovereigns, she concluded that it would be safe to proceed.

The party accordingly went to the station that very afternoon and took passage for Carlisle, a town near the frontier of Scotland, and on the way to Glasgow.

CHAPTER IX.

THE RAILWAY RIDE.

"Now, Florence," said Grimkie, when the cab arrived at the station, and stopped for the party to get out, "now we shall see which is the best —an English railroad ride, or an American one."

A man in a peculiar velveteen dress of a bronze green color, and with a badge upon his arm to mark his official character, came with a barrow, and in a very respectful manner asked where the party were going.

"To Carlisle," said Grimkie.

"Very well," said the man. "If you will follow me to the platform I will show you where to get the tickets."

So saying the porter put the trunks and all the parcels carefully upon his barrow, and led the way through an arched passage into the interior of the station. Grimkie paid the cabman, and then, with the rest of the party, followed the porter.

When they entered the station, a remarkable scene presented itself to view. Florence looked about with great surprise and admiration. She saw an immense space covered with a glass roof, with platforms flagged with stone along the sides, and great numbers of trains on the different tracks in the center. Great hissing locomotives were moving to and fro, on these tracks, and parties of travellers, with porters wheeling their trunks and parcels on their barrows, were moving in various directions along the platforms. There were doors opening into pretty rooms, with signs over them, marked, First Class Waiting Rooms, and Second Class Waiting Rooms, and First Class Refreshment Rooms, and the like. One of the objects which most strongly attracted Florence's attention, was a very elegant little book stall, with a great variety of entertaining books displayed on the shelves of it, together with prints, newspapers and periodicals, all neatly arranged on open shelves, or behind glass sashes.

But there was not time to stop and look at these things, for the porter went on, and it seemed necessary to follow him. He took the barrow near to one of the trains which was standing upon the track, and stopping there, he said to Grimkie,

"You have plenty of time, sir. The train does not go for twenty minutes. Your luggage will be quite safe here, and if you will come with me I will show you the waiting-room, and then I will come and tell you when it is time to get the tickets."

"Can't I get the tickets now?" asked Grimkie.

"Not quite yet, sir," said the porter. "The ticket office for this train will be open in about ten minutes."

So saying, the porter led the way to the first class waiting room, and the whole party went in. They found a spacious and handsomely furnished room, with a great table in the center, and very comfortable-looking sofas and arm-chairs against the walls. On one side was a door opening into the refreshment room, where they saw a large table elegantly set, as if for a sumptuous dinner. Beyond was a counter loaded with decanters, plates of fruits, tarts, pies, and all sorts of delicacies, and with one or two very tidy-looking girls behind it, ready to wait upon customers.

"What nice rooms!" said Florence.

"Yes," said Grimkie. "These are for the first class passengers."

"How did the porter know that we were going first class?" asked Florence.

"He knew by our looks," said Grimkie; "besides, he knew by our being Americans. Americans always take the first class. They don't go for marking themselves publicly as second rate people, and so whether they are rich or poor, they all rush into the first class carriages."

"Who told you that?" asked Florence. Florence knew very well that Grimkie was quoting what somebody else had said, for the language did not sound at all as if it were original with him.

"A gentleman on board the steamer," said Grimkie, coolly.

"Mother," said Florence, turning to Mrs. Morelle, who had seated herself comfortably upon one of the sofas, "let us go out on the platform again. It is a great deal more amusing there than here."

"I think so, too," said Mrs. Morelle. So saying, she rose from her seat, and they all went together out upon the platform, and began to walk up and down, amusing themselves with observing what was going on. Grimkie and John began to read the placards and notices which were posted up along the walls. Some of them were adorned with pictures printed in colored inks, and were mounted in handsome frames.

While they were looking at these things, the porter came again and told Grimkie that the ticket office was now open, and he proceeded to show him the way to it. Grimkie bought the tickets, and then the porter led the way toward the night train. Mrs. Morelle and John went on together after him, and Grimkie and Florence followed.

"This is very nice," said Florence, "to have a man wait upon us in this way, and show us exactly what we are to do."

"Yes," said Grimkie, "but then we have to pay for it."

"No," replied Florence, "for I saw a notice posted up that the men were not allowed to receive anything whatever from the passengers. If they do take anything they are to be dismissed."

"I don't mean that we have to pay the *men*," said Grimkie, "but the *company*. The fares are a great deal higher in England than in America. Here they have plenty of servants to wait upon us at the stations, and they charge accordingly. In America every man takes care of himself and saves his money."

"Not all of it," said Florence.

"No, not all of it," replied Grimkie, "but all that part which the company would require to employ servants at all the stations to take care of him. Besides, this porter will expect a sixpence from me, and I have got one all ready to give to him. You will see how he will manage to get it slily. The gentleman on board the steamer told me all about it."

By this time the porter had come to the train. The train was not composed, as in America, of a few long cars, but of a larger number of carriages, each of which contained three separate compartments, with doors at the sides. The porter went to one of these carriages, marked First Class, and opened the door. Grimkie put in some of the small parcels of the luggage, and the porter put the trunks upon the top. He kept one bag in his hands and told Grimkie that he would hand it to him after he got in. So Grimkie got into the carriage and took his seat, and the porter, after he had put up the trunks upon the top, within the railing which had been made there to keep them from falling off, and had covered them with a tarpaulin, took the bag and put it into the carriage, contriving at the same time, when he shut the door, to hold his hand inside of it a moment, in such a way that Grimkie could give him the sixpence.

"You will not change carriages, sir," said he to Grimkie, "until you get to Carlisle, and then you will find your luggage on the top quite safe."

"Grimkie," said Florence, as soon as the man had gone. "You ought not to have given that man a sixpence. He is liable to lose his place for taking it."

"Yes," said Grimkie. "Provided any body saw him take it."

"That makes no difference," said Florence, "whether any body saw him take it or not. It makes not the least difference in the world. You have broken the law."

"No," said Grimkie. "*I* have not broken any law. There is no law against the traveller's giving the sixpence, but only against the porter's taking it. *He* may have broken a law, but I have not."

"Oh Grimkie!" said Florence.

Florence was no match for Grimkie in the logical management of an argument, and she did not know exactly how to reply to his reasoning in this instance, though she felt very confident that he was wrong. Her thoughts were, however, for the present, at once diverted from the subject, for the train began to move, and in a very few minutes it appeared that it was entering a dark tunnel. The interior of the carriage, however, did not become dark, for in proportion as the daylight faded away the illumination which it had produced was replaced by a lamp-light which gradually began to appear. Where this lamp-light could come from was at first a mystery, but, on looking up, the children saw a lamp burning brightly in a glass which was set into the top of the carriage over their heads, with a reflector above it which threw the light down. This light made it very cheerful and pleasant within the car while the train was passing the tunnel.

On emerging from the tunnel at the other end a marvelous picture of verdure and beauty met the view of the travellers, and filled them with delight. Florence particularly was charmed with the aspect of the scene. She looked out first at one window and then the other, scarcely knowing which way to turn in her fear that something would escape her. The rich and deep green of the fields, the hawthorn hedges, in full flower, the gardens, the beautiful villas, the charming cottages, half covered with eglantine and ivy, the little railway stations, which the train passed from time to time, built substantially of stone, in very picturesque and endlessly varied forms, and with the prettiest ornamental gardens which can be imagined surrounding them, or extending from them each way along the sloping banks which bordered the track—these and a hundred other objects which came into view in the most rapid and ever changing succession, kept her in a continual state of excitement.

It was about one o'clock when the train left

Liverpool, and it reached Carlisle about half past five. The distance was about a hundred and thirty miles. The time passed, however, very rapidly. A short time before the train arrived, Mrs. Morelle asked Grimkie what he was going to do about a hotel.

"You know," said she, "that the agreement is that you are to take the whole care of the party, just as if you were my courier."

A courier is a travelling servant, who is employed by a gentleman travelling, or by a lady, or a family, to conduct them wherever they wish to go on their journey. He takes care of all the luggage, knows which are the good hotels, makes bargains with the keepers of them, and settles the bills, makes arrangements for horses and carriages when travelling, and in a word relieves his employers of all trouble and care, and enables them to make their journey with as much ease and quiet of mind as if they were merely taking a morning's drive on their own grounds at home.

That is to say, this is the case when the employer of the courier understands how to manage properly. It is with travelling couriers as with all other servants; every thing depends upon the principles of management adopted by the master or mistress. A courier is a means of great convenience and comfort in travelling, or a source of continual vexation and trouble, according to the tact or want of tact displayed by the traveller himself, in employing and directing him.

Grimkie looked a little at a loss when his aunt asked him what hotel he was going to. He said he had intended to have asked some gentleman in the cars, supposing that the cars would be large, as in America, and that there would be a great many people in them. But in fact there had been no one in their compartment of the carriage all the way. He had looked into his guide book, and the guide book gave the names of two or three of the hotels in Carlisle, but did not say which was the best.

"Read us the names, Grimkie," said Florence. "We can judge something by the sound of them."

So Grimkie opened the book and began to read.

"There's the Royal Hotel," said he.

"We won't go there," said John, "at any rate. We are republicans."

"And there's a hotel called the County Hotel," continued Grimkie. "It is in the station."

"In the station?" repeated Florence; "let us go there. It will seem very funny to be at a hotel that is in the station. May we go to any hotel that we choose, mother?"

"You may go to any one that Grimkie chooses," replied Mrs. Morelle. "He is responsible for finding us comfortable quarters for the night."

"I'll see how the station hotel looks when we get there," said Grimkie to Florence, "and if it looks pleasant we will stop there."

This plan for deciding the question in respect to the Station Hotel seemed to be in theory a very good one, but it proved unfortunately impracticable, for when the train stopped, and Grimkie had helped his party out from the carriage to the platform, he found no signs of the hotel to be seen, except two or three porters who wore the badges of the hotel upon their caps, and one of whom stood ready at once to take charge of Grimkie's luggage and to show the way to the hotel. Grimkie, who had no time for reflection, decided at once to accept the offer, and as soon as the trunks were handed down and put upon the hotel porter's barrow, he followed with Mrs. Morelle and the children where the porter led.

They went for some distance along the platform, and then turned to a side door which led to a long passage gently ascending. At the end of this passage they ascended some steps and entered a door, and there turning to the left they came into another long passage which looked like the entry of the hotel. Apartments of various kinds opened from it on each side, and waiters were seen carrying dinners and suppers to the different rooms. At the end of this passage was a sort of office, and turning round the corner an elegant stair-case came into view, leading to the stories above. A pretty looking young woman met the party at the office door. Grimkie said they wanted a sitting-room and two bed-rooms. The young woman led the way up stairs to show the rooms.

In about half an hour after this time the whole party were sitting down, in excellent spirits, and with great appetites, to a very nice dinner, in an elegant little room, with windows looking out upon a great area filled with omnibuses and cabs that were waiting for the arrival of the next train, and upon a street which passed by a spacious castle-like building that seemed to stand at the entrance to the town.

After dinner they all went out to take a walk. On entering the town they found themselves in a narrow street with very ancient but very solid and substantial looking buildings on either side of it, the whole entirely unlike any thing which they had ever seen in America. They passed by several inns which were so quaint and curious in their structure, and looked so snug and so neat, and so much like the representations of English inns which they had seen in pictures and drawing-books, that Florence began to be sorry that they had stopped at the Station Hotel, which was modern and new, and the rooms in which were very much like those of a nice hotel in America.

"Grimkie," said she, "we made a mistake. We ought to have come to one of these little old fashioned inns here in the town. See what nice curtains at the chamber windows. If we had only known about these."

"Ah yes," said Grimkie. "If we could only manage when we are coming into a strange town, to have a chance to see all the hotels and inns beforehand, we could choose a great deal better."

"You made a great mistake this time," said Florence.

"Next time then *you* shall choose," said Grimkie.

Florence was prepared for some sort of tart reply from Grimkie, to her finding fault with him, but when she heard so kind and polite a reply, it produced a reaction in her own feelings. After a moment's pause she said,

"Grimkie, it was *I* that chose this time.

Going to the Station Hotel was my plan, after all."

"Was it?" said Grimkie; "well you shall choose the next time too, if you like."

The principal object of the walk which our party were taking at this time, was to visit the Cathedral of Carlisle. It was the first cathedral which the children had had an opportunity of seeing. They found a very ancient and venerable pile, with ruins around it, and several little streets, and open spaces, with pretty houses fronting them, all of which seemed to belong to the cathedral, for they were enclosed with it in a wall which separated the whole precinct from the rest of the town. This precinct is called the cathedral close. It pertains exclusively to the cathedral, and is under ecclesiastical jurisdiction, in a measure, and contains the dwellings of the various clergymen and laymen that are attached to the cathedral service.

There was a certain air of solemn stillness and repose reigning about the precincts of the cathedral, when our party entered the close, which was very impressive. The venerable walls of the cathedral itself crumbling with age, the old inscriptions and sculptured images, now in some cases almost wholly effaced by the decay of the stone,—the masses of ruined walls, the remains of ancient cloisters or chapels which were seen here and there rising from the patches of greensward,—the smooth and solitary walks—and above all the mournful chirping of the rooks and swallows and daws that were flying about among the turrets and parapets far above, or in the tops of the ancient trees—combined to impart a peculiar expression of solemn and melancholy grandeur to the scene, which was wholly indescribable.

After rambling about the town and the environs till after ten o'clock, the party returned to the Station Hotel, where they all went to bed without candles, for it was not yet dark.

The next morning, soon after breakfast, Grimkie paid the bill, and they all went down to the platform to take the train which was to leave about half-past eight o'clock for Glasgow. They were soon all comfortably seated in the carriage, and five minutes afterward the train was in motion. They had a delightful journey to Glasgow, where they arrived safely a little after noon.

CHAPTER X.

THE HIGHLAND GLENS.

"Now," said Grimkie, when the party arrived at the hotel in Glasgow, "we have come to the end of the first stage of our journey, that is the railway stage of it. The next is the steamboat stage."

"I am glad of that," said Florence. "The railway ride was very pleasant, but I am ready for a change."

Grimkie had learned in the course of the conversations which he had held with his fellow-passengers on board the ship at sea, that it was best, in travelling in Scotland, especially among the Highlands, to take as little baggage as possible.

"On whichever side of Scotland you go up," said one of these gentlemen, "you will be likely to come down on the other side, so that your journey will either begin at Glasgow and end at Edinburgh, or it will begin at Edinburgh and end at Glasgow. You will find it better therefore, when you are ready to set out from either of those towns, to put all that you will want for the journey in one trunk, and send all the rest of your baggage across to some hotel in the other town, to wait there for you till you come back."

Grimkie explained all this to his aunt, at the breakfast table at their hotel in Glasgow. Mrs. Morelle looked at her travelling map of Scotland, and she saw that Edinburgh and Glasgow were in fact situated as is represented above.

"We shall probably come down from the Orkneys on that side of the island," said she, "and I think it would be convenient to have our trunks go there, all except one—but then, Grimkie, we don't know how to send them there. I suppose there is some kind of express, if we only knew where the office was."

"Ah," but you remember, Auntie, that father told us that all we had to do was to be able to tell distinctly what we wanted, and the people here would find out how it was to be done."

"That was in the public offices," said Mrs. Morelle.

"It will do just as well in the hotels I expect, Auntie," said Grimkie. "May I ring the bell and try?"

Mrs. Morelle gave the required permission, and Grimkie rang the bell. Very soon the waiter appeared.

"I want to see about sending some baggage to Edinburgh," said Grimkie.

"Yes, sir," said the waiter. "I'll send up Boots directly."

Boots is the familiar name by which the porter is designated in the English inns. In these inns moreover every servant has his own definite duties to perform, and these are never on any account intermingled. It is the porter's duty to know about railway trains, and conveyances of all kinds, and about baggage, and sending letters and parcels, and all such things. The waiter's duty, on the other hand, is confined entirely to the service of the table, and to acts of personal attendance upon the guests within the hotel. If any question arises pertaining to transportation or conveyance of any kind, he has but one answer—"Yes, sir. I'll send Boots."

In a few minutes the porter appeared, cap in hand.

"We want to inquire about sending some of our luggage to Edinburgh," said Grimkie. "We are going to make a tour in the north of Scotland, and we thought it would be best to send most of our luggage to Edinburgh to wait there till we come."

"Yes, sir," said the porter, "that will be much the best way for you."

"And how shall we manage it?" asked Grimkie. "What have I to do?"

"You have nothing at all to do," said the porter," except to tell me the name of the hotel where you will go—or put it upon your luggage, and leave it in your room here when you go away. I will attend to it all, and you will find it quite safe at the hotel when you arrive there."

"And how about paying?" asked Grimkie. "Shall we pay you?"

"No, sir," said the porter, "you will have nothing to pay here. It will not be much, and they will pay at the hotel in Edinburgh and put it in your bill."

"That will be exactly the thing, Auntie," said Grimkie. "Only," he added, "we do not know what hotel we shall go to."

On being asked by Mrs. Morelle, the porter gave them the address of a good hotel in Edinburgh, which he said was in a pleasant situation, and a well kept house. He also brought Grimkie a package of gum labels, such as are used in England for labelling baggage. Grimkie wrote Mrs. Morelle's name on several of these labels, and also the name of the hotel which the porter had given him, and then, after his aunt had selected from all the trunks what she thought would be required for the whole party during the tour in Scotland, and had put them in the one which she was to take, Grimkie with the assistance of the porter locked and strapped the others, and put the labels upon them.

The party spent the rest of the day in rambling about Glasgow, and in amusing themselves with the various objects of interest which met their view in the streets and in the environs, and the next morning before breakfast, they went on board the steamer Iona, which was to take them to Inverness.

They enjoyed the voyage exceedingly although at first Florence was somewhat disappointed in respect to the steamer, which she had expected would be as much superior, in respect to its size, and its decorations, to those plying upon the North River, as Europe is generally considered superior to America. Instead of this, the Iona was comparatively quite small, but it was very neatly arranged, and there was a small, but richly furnished cabin below, which looked exceedingly snug and comfortable.

After rambling about the steamer until they had explored it in every part, the children went with Mrs. Morelle and chose a place upon the deck at a corner near the companion-way, where they could enjoy the views on every side, and at the same time, could be comfortably seated all

ON BOARD THE IONA.

the time, if they chose, on camp-stools and benches.

Here they remained for several hours enjoying the most charming succession of views of mountain scenery that can be imagined. Grimkie, by means of the maps and guide books, followed the course of the steamer, and found out the names of all the villages, and castles, and country seats, which came successively into view, and pointed them out to his aunt and Florence who examined them attentively, especially the old castles, by means of the opera glass.

The course of the steamer lay through a succession of channels, lakes and sounds, most of which were connected with the sea, but they were so hemmed in by the promontories and islands which bordered them, as to make it seem to the party as if they were navigating inland waters altogether. The channels of water were so narrow too, in most cases, that the land was very near. It was generally more like sailing upon a river, than upon an arm of the sea. The land was everywhere very mountainous too, and seemed to rise very abruptly from the water's edge, though often it was bordered near the margin of the water, by villages and towns, and elegant country seats with green fields and beautiful gardens adjoining them, and parks and pleasure grounds, all of which presented a succession of most charming pictures to the view.

In other places the shores of the *loch*, as the Scotch call such sheets of water as these, were wild and solitary,—immense sheep pastures extending up the mountain sides to a great height, with flocks of sheep, and dogs, and Highland shepherds seen here and there, standing motionless to gaze upon the steamer as it glided swiftly by.

As this line of steamers was intended almost exclusively for the accommodation of tourists, journeying for health or pleasure, the arrangements on board were all made with reference to rendering the voyage as comfortable and as agreeable as possible. One of the arrangements made with this view was to stop at night, half way between Glasgow and Inverness, at a place situated in the midst of some of the grandest and most romantic scenery, in order to give the passengers a quiet night's sleep, at a spacious and elegant hotel, built there expressly for the purpose. The steamer was to touch too at a great many different places along the route, wherever there was a pretty village on the margin of the water, or any grand or picturesque scenery at a little distance in the interior. When Mrs. Morelle and her party came on board, they had not determined whether to proceed directly to Inverness, or to stop at Rothsay, or Oban, or Fort William, or at some other interesting point, with a view of continuing their journey on a subsequent day.

"We will not decide," said Mrs. Morelle, "until we get on board the steamer, and see how we like it, and what the weather is."

When, however, the party had embarked and the voyage was begun, they were all for the first hour so much interested in the wonderful beauty and grandeur of the scenery which everywhere met their view, that they did not think of the question how far they should go, until Grimkie saw the man coming round among the passengers to receive their money, and give them tickets. Before he had time to say anything about it, the man came to where Mrs. Morelle was sitting and said he would take the fare.

"How much is it, sir?" asked Grimkie.

The man replied by asking how far they were going. Grimkie looked to his aunt, not knowing himself exactly what to say.

"We are going to Inverness," said she, "but we had not fully decided whether to go directly through, or to stop somewhere, for a day."

"You can pay through, madam," said the man, "and take a ticket, and then you can break the journey where you please. The tickets are good for a month."

"Ah," said Grimkie, "that will be just the thing for us." So he took out his purse and counted out the number of sovereigns which the man required, and received the tickets.

The tickets were made in a very curious manner. They were printed upon thin paper, and lined upon the back with green morocco, and were then folded in three, that is, the upper part was folded down, and the lower part up, and in this condition they looked like so many little green wallets. Florence and John were very much interested in examining their tickets, and they wished to have the custody of them themselves. But Grimkie said no. He was responsible for all the payments, and he must take charge of the tickets himself—but they might have them to look at as often as they pleased.

John was very much taken with the ticket man's phrase "break the journey," and he began to be quite desirous that *their* journey should be broken at some point or other along the route. His mother said that she had no objection to that. So she commissioned Grimkie to look over the map and the guide books, and read the descriptions of the different places along the route, and of the objects of interest to be seen in the vicinity of them, and so select a place where in his opinion it would be best to stop.

Grimkie immediately set himself to this work, and after a good deal of patient investigation and research, he came to the conclusion to recommend that they should stop at Ben Nevis. Ben Nevis, he found, lay close upon their course.

Ben Nevis has usually been considered as the highest mountain in Scotland. It is any rate altogether the most celebrated. There is a little village at the base of it, named Fort William, where travellers land who wish to ascend the mountain. This village is at the head of a loch, and all the environs of it are romantic and beautiful. Grimkie found a picture of Fort William in one of the guide books, and showed it to his aunt, and to Florence and John. He also read what the guide book said about the place, and the environs of it, and the mode of ascending the mountain.

"I have only one objection to stopping there," said Mrs. Morelle, "and that is that I do not like climbing mountains very well."

"But, Auntie," said Grimkie, "we need not go up the mountain unless we choose to do it."

"True," said Mrs. Morelle, "but I am pretty sure you children will want to go up, and I shall not like to have you go, unless I go too."

"Then, Auntie, how would you like to stop at Oban?"

"What is there remarkable at Oban?" asked Mrs. Morelle.

"It is a pretty little town on the western coast, built along the curve of a bay, under high hills," said Grimkie, half reading from his guide book. "It is a sort of central point and rendezvous for travellers in the western Highlands, being the place of departure for many excursions."

"What sort of excursions?" asked Mrs. Morelle.

"The principal are steamboat excursions among the outlying islands," said Grimkie, "such as to Fingal's cave on the island of Staffa, and the old monastery in Iona."

"Should we be exposed to the swell of the sea in going to those islands?" asked Mrs. Morelle.

"I think from the map that we should," said Grimkie.

"Then," said Mrs. Morelle, laughing, "I would rather stop at Ben Nevis. I would rather take the mountain than the sea."

"I thought so, Auntie," said Grimkie.

And so it was decided that the party should land at Fort William, at the base of Ben Nevis.

CHAPTER XI.

BEN NEVIS.

Mrs. Morelle was charmed with the appearance of Ben Nevis and its environs when the steamer drew near. The slopes of the mountain seemed to commence almost at the margin of the water, and they rose in solemn grandeur to a vast height, the portions near the summit being covered with great patches of snow. Lower down, the mountain sides were rounded and smooth, and covered with rich green and brown vegetation, which glowed in the setting sun and seemed as soft as the richest velvet. Along the margin of the water were extended the buildings of the town, with vessels of various size lying at anchor near.

The steamer stopped at some distance from the shore, just as Grimkie and John, who had been forward to see about getting out the trunk, came back to see if Mrs. Morelle and Florence were ready. Mrs. Morelle looked alarmed.

"Why, Grimkie!" said she, "are they going

to land us in a boat. I thought they would go up to the pier. I am afraid to land in a boat."

"Then we can go on," said Grimkie, "to the end of the sail. It is not a great deal farther."

"But I should like to stop and see Ben Nevis, too," said Mrs. Morelle hesitating—"if it were not for landing in a boat—going down such a steep and narrow ladder."

"There can't be any real danger, Auntie," said Grimkie, "but still we will go on if you prefer. They land by boats at half the places where we stop."

This was very true, and Mrs. Morelle had taken great interest in watching the progress of such landings, several times during the day. It was very curious to see the boat in such cases come out from the land, and lie upon its oars on the water in the track of the steamer, until the steamer came up, and the paddle-wheels were backed. Then the man standing on the guard would throw a rope to the boat, which would be caught by a man at the bows of it, and immediately made fast, by which means the boat would be drawn on through the water, by the steamer which was not yet entirely at rest.

The boat was soon pulled in under the little step-ladder leading from the deck, which had previously been let down, and then the passengers who were to land would descend, guarded carefully, by strong boatmen reaching up from the boat to the outer side of the ladder, to prevent the possibility of their falling into the water, in case of any misstep.

As fast as the passengers reached the boat, they stepped over the thwarts and took their seats in the stern. Then the trunks and other parcels of baggage were passed down. Then the boatmen would take the oars again, the rope was cast off, the boat was pushed away, the paddle-wheels recommenced their motion, and the steamer went on, leaving the boat behind to struggle with the waves as best it could, and make its slow way to the shore.

All this had been very interesting to see, as it appeared to the passengers who stood leaning over the bulwarks and looking down upon it from the deck above, but Mrs. Morelle thought that it would not be very agreeable to go through. She was afraid, in the first place, to go down such a steep and narrow ladder, especially when the resting place was so unstable and insecure at the bottom. Then she was still more afraid of the pitching and tossing of the boat, in the surges made by the paddle-wheels when the steamer moved away.

She did not, however, hesitate long, for a moment's reflection convinced her that these fears were imaginary. There could not possibly be any real danger in the mode of landing adopted, as the ordinary and usual method for such a class of travellers as those on board this steamer. So she banished her fears, and rising from her seat, said that she would go.

By this time the boat had made fast along side the steamer, and the passengers who were to go on shore were going down the ladder. Mrs. Morelle found no difficulty in following them, Florence and John followed her. Grimkie remained at the head of the ladder to the last. When all had descended that were going, the trunks were put down, and then the boat pushed off, and the steamer resumed her voyage.*

The next morning, while at breakfast at the inn at Fort William, Grimkie proposed to his aunt that they should all make an excursion up the mountain.

"Not to the top of it, Auntie," said he, "but only so far as you find you will like to go. We will get a guide and set off together. We will ride to the foot of the mountain. Then we will begin to walk up. You shall go first and we will follow you, and we will not ask to go any farther than you like. We will go as slowly,

* See Frontispiece.

and stop to rest as often, as you please ; and then when we get high enough for a good view, we can turn about and come back again."

There could of course be no objection to so exceedingly reasonable a proposal as this, and Mrs. Morelle said at once that she should like to make an excursion up the mountain, on those conditions, very much indeed.

"If I walk slowly," said she, "I can walk two hours."

"That will take us up pretty high," said Grimkie. "It only takes two hours and a half to get to the top. So you and Florence may get ready Auntie, and John and I will go down and see about a carriage and a guide."

The usual mode would have been for Grimkie to have rung the bell and called for Boots, and so have made the arrangement for the carriage and the guide through him. But there were some preparations that he wished to make secretly, and so he left his aunt and Florence, and went down to the coffee-room of the hotel. He took his seat there at one of the tables, near a window, and asked the waiter to send Boots in to him.

When Boots came, Grimkie told him that they were going a little way up the mountain, and made an arrangement with him to have a dog-cart got ready immediately, to take them as far as they could go in a carriage, and also to engage a guide, and to send the guide in to the coffee-room to see him. In a few minutes the guide came.

He was a nice tidy-looking young man, with a frank and good-humored countenance, and a broad Scotch accent in his speech. Grimkie explained the case to him.

"We are going up the mountain a little way," said Grimkie. "We want to go as far as we can, but my aunt is not used to climbing mountains much, and so we must go very slowly."

"Oh, aye," said the guide, "the slower ye gang, the higher oop y'ell get."

The guide had had great experience with travelling parties attempting to ascend the mountain, and he had known many ladies to become tired and discouraged before reaching the top, just because they could not be contented to go slowly enough at the beginning.

After some further discussion and consultation, the plan for the excursion was matured in all its details. The guide was to go forward on foot, carrying with him a supply of provisions which Grimkie was to have made ready, and to wait at the end of the carriage road until the party in the carriage should come up. The provisions—

which the waiter at the coffee-room subsequently made ready under Grimkie's directions—consisted of a bottle of coffee, another of milk, a cold roast chicken, some sandwiches, two buttered rolls, a little paper of salt, one plate, one knife, four forks, and a tumbler. All these the waiter packed carefully in two round wooden boxes, and put the boxes in a bag. That was the way he said that the guides liked to have their burdens packed.

The bag thus arranged was to be put into the dog-cart, to be carried in that way as far the cart could go, with a view of being taken by the guide there, and carried by him over his shoulder for the rest of the ascent.

When Grimkie had completed these arrangements he went up to his aunt's room again, and there he found John who had gone up a moment before him, remonstrating in a somewhat urgent manner with Florence against a plan which she entertained of carrying a large guide book up the mountain, to press flowers in.

"You can't carry such a big book as that," said John. "It's ridiculous. We must have every thing as light as possible, in going up a mountain. Grimkie says so."

"But this is the only book I have got," said Florence, "and I must take some book. It is very important for me to get some specimens from Ben Nevis, to carry home for souvenirs."

"Then you must bring them down in your hand," said John. "We can't possibly take such a big book as that; can we Grimkie?"

"I will see about that presently," said Grimkie. "Come with me, John. I want you to go somewhere."

So John laid down the big book and followed Grimkie down stairs. Grimkie led the way into the street.

"Where are you going, Grimkie?" asked John.

"I am going to see if I can find a bookseller," said Grimkie. "But you should not contradict a young lady in that short way. That's boyish."

"How boyish?" said John.

"Why boys fly in their sisters' faces in that way sometimes, but no gentleman ever does."

"But Grimkie," said John, "it is perfectly ridiculous to think of carrying such a big book as that up a high mountain."

"That's the very reason why you ought to be more gentle in setting her right," replied Grimkie. "Do you think a lady likes to have it made to appear to her face that any thing she says or does is ridiculous?"

"Then what shall I do?" asked John.

"You must be more gentle," said Grimkie.

"A lady is like a steamboat; you can't turn her short about, by a sudden twitch, when she is going wrong. You must bring her round by a sweep—in a grand circle—gently and gracefully. I'll show you how."

By this time the boys arrived at the door of a small bookstore, and Grimkie immediately went in. John followed him. Grimkie asked a young woman who stood behind the counter if she had any blotting paper. She immediately produced half a quire, and Grimkie bought six sheets of it. These sheets he cut in two with a paper knife, and then after folding them, cut them again. He then folded them again, thus bringing them into a snug compass for carrying, that is, as the bookbinders would say, into an *octavo* form. The paper as it was when he bought it, was in a folio form. After he had cut and folded it the first time, it was in a quarto form, and now after a second folding, by which means each sheet formed eight leaves, it was put into the octavo form. Another folding still, which would have made sixteen leaves to the sheet, would have produced what is called the sixteenmo form.

Grimkie and John immediately returned to the hotel, carrying the paper with them. As soon as they arrived, Grimkie went to his room and took a small portfolio off his table. This portfolio was simply the cover of a blank book Grimkie had used at the Chateau for some of his exercises. When it was full and he had no further occasion to use it, he had cut out the inside neatly, in order to save the cover, which was quite a pretty one, being made of green morocco. He thought it would make a nice portfolio. He had accordingly stocked it with small note papers and envelopes, and had made it serve the purpose of a stationery case, for his travels.

He now took out the note paper and his envelopes from it, and then compared the blotting-paper in its octavo form with the size of the cover. He found that by folding it once more, that is into the sixteenmo form, it would fit the cover very well. So he cut it open at the octavo folding, and then after folding it again he slipped it into the cover and went to find Florence.

"Florence," said he, "how do you think this will do to put your little flowers in up the mountain? It is made of blotting paper, and that is much better than the paper of books to press plants in, for it absorbs the moisture, and so dries the plants quicker, and that makes them preserve their colors better."

"That will be excellent," said Florence, taking the book and looking at it with great interest. "But how did you know about that?"

"Our professor of botany at the Chateau," said Grimkie, "told us that it is better to have a book made of blotting paper. Only this book is not sewed. Could you sew it?"

"I can sew it in a moment," said Florence.

"Then it will do nicely," said Grimkie. "If you can sew the leaves together so as to make a book of them, then we can slip them into the book cover, and that will be all we shall want. I can carry it in my pocket. You see you don't want large specimens. The smaller and more delicate they are the better. Our professor told us that."

"Your professor?" repeated Florence.

"Yes," replied Grimkie; "he lectured us about it. 'Young gentlemen,' said he, 'the mode of procedure is very different both in the selection of flowers and in the method of preserving them, according to the object you have in view, whether to procure botanical specimens for purposes of science, or souvenirs and tokens for purposes of sentiment and love.'"

Grimkie repeated these words in a tone and manner imitative of a lecturer making a discourse before an audience, producing thus a very comical effect, so that both John and Florence laughed outright.

"Oh, Grimkie!" exclaimed Florence.

"I don't believe he said any such things," added John.

"He verily did," replied Grimkie. 'Young gentlemen,' said he, 'when you have advanced a little farther along the verdant and flowery path of life, you will sometimes have occasion, in your various wanderings, to prepare plants and flowers as tokens of remembrance, or of other sentiments, or as souvenirs of travel. In such cases, gentlemen, select small and delicate specimens—of graceful forms and pretty colors. Press them till they are dry between leaves of blotting paper. If necessary, separate the leaves and stems so as to press and preserve them separately. You can recompose your flower afterward. Examine the specimens from time to time while they are drying, and see that the stems lie in natural and graceful curves, and that the leaves and petals are smooth, and fully extended. Then when they are thoroughly dry, arrange the parts anew, and gum them delicately upon a small piece of white paper, with a suitable inscription beneath, and enclose the paper in a tinted envelope of the right size to contain it,—and then when you present it to the Mary, or the Lucy, or the Ellen, for whom it is intended, she will perceive that you are a young gentleman of taste and skill, as well as of science.'"

Grimkie finished this recitation of a portion of the professor's lecture with such an air of mock gravity, that Florence and John both laughed louder than ever.

"Oh, Grimkie!" said John, "did the professor really say that?"

"Yes," said Grimkie, "and we all clapped him."

"It seems to me you have pretty funny doings at the Chateau, Grimkie," said Florence.

"We do sometimes," said Grimkie. "But hark!" he added, "I thought I heard wheels coming. No they are not coming yet, but we must not waste any more time. We must get ready. The dog-cart will be here very soon."

"Good!" said John, at the same time cutting a caper, to express his joy.

"But what kind of dogs will they be?" he added, turning to Grimkie. "Will they be Esquimaux dogs?"

"There they come," said Grimkie; "run to the window and see."

John supposed that a dog-cart was a cart made to be *drawn* by dogs. In this idea he was greatly mistaken, a dog-cart being made to *carry* dogs, and not to be drawn by them. It is quite a curious vehicle, having its origin in the wish of sportsmen to provide some means of transporting their dogs, as well as themselves and their guns, when going into the field, so that the dogs may be fresh and in good condition for their work, when they arrive there.

It is a very handsomely made vehicle, in the form of a cart. The seat is double, there being places for two persons to sit on the front part, facing the horse, and two directly behind them, with their backs against those of the first two. Underneath this double seat is a box or recess, for the dogs. The lid which shuts this box, is behind, and is made to open down in such a manner that when it is opened it is sustained by a support which holds it in nearly a horizontal position, where it forms a foot-board for the two persons riding behind to rest their feet upon.

The children were all very much interested in examining the form and construction of the dog-cart when they went down to the door. The coachman took the right hand front seat. Mrs. Morelle took the other front seat. John and Florence and Grimkie took the seat behind, where they were so much crowded at first, that John said he had a great mind to play that he was a pointer or a setter, and crawl into the box below.

After having been shaken together a little while by the jolting of the carriage—for a dog-cart moves, even upon a smooth road, with a very jerking and jolting motion—they found themselves quite comfortable, and they had a very amusing ride.

When they reached the end of the carriage-road, they found a guide there ready for them. He took the bag containing the provisions, from the fore part of the dog-cart where the coachman had put it, and threw it over his shoulder, in such a manner that one of the boxes hung down before him, and the other behind. The coachman then took the dog-cart to a farmer's near by, to put up the horse, to wait until the party returned, while the guide, followed by his party, commenced his ascent of the mountain.

The path was very good, although rather rugged and steep, but the country was open, there being in general no trees, but only furze, broom, whinbushes, and other such shrubs as grow upon the Scottish Highlands. Grimkie wished very much that his aunt should ascend to the top of the mountain, but he knew very well that the only hope of her being able to do so, must depend upon their going very slowly at first. John and Florence who both felt very fresh and agile, were eager to press forward, but Grimkie kept them back, stopping continually to gather flowers, and to look back at the prospect. Whenever he found a flat stone with a smooth and clear surface, he persuaded his aunt to sit down, and when she was once seated, he detained her as long as possible, by talking with her, and amusing her mind with the objects around her. Then he would point to the next elevation above, and ask his aunt if she thought she could go up to it; and she would say, "Oh, yes! I am not tired at all yet."

In this way the party sauntered along for more than three hours, advancing all the time, but in a slow and unconcerned manner, without thought or care, as if they were out for a walk, without any definite plan in respect to the end of the excursion. At last, however, about noon, Mrs. Morelle took out her watch, and expressed surprise to find how late it was, and said that it was time for her to begin to think about going home.

"Look up there, Auntie," said Grimkie, "where that shepherd is standing with his dog. There must be a grand lookout from there. Let us go up as high as that, and there we will have our luncheon, and then, if you please, we will set out for home."

Mrs. Morelle made no objection to going up

to the point which Grimkie had indicated, and they soon attained it. Here they found a spring of water coming out from under a great rock. Grimkie brought some flat stones and made seats for the party in a shady and sheltered place, and then the guide opened the bag and took out the provisions. Mrs. Morelle was quite surprised to see so abundant a supply of provisions coming to view.

"I did not know that we were going to have even a luncheon on the mountain," said she, "and here you have got enough, almost, for a dinner."

The party remained at the spring for more than half an hour, and then Mrs. Morelle found herself so much refreshed by the chicken and the sandwiches, and especially by the tumbler of cold coffee which Grimkie mixed for her, that she said she was almost inclined to go on farther; and when the guide told her that an hour more of easy walking would bring her to the very top, she said she had half a mind to try to go there.

"Do you think I could do it, Grimkie?" said she.

Grimkie said it was a great thing for a lady to get to the top of Ben Nevis, but if she felt strong enough to try it, he should like it very much indeed. She might go on for half an hour more at any rate, and then if she felt tired she could turn.

Mrs. Morelle determined to follow this suggestion, and the result was, that she persevered until she reached the top.

The wind blew very fresh and cool upon the summit, and the party could not remain there long. While they did remain, however, they were filled with wonder and delight at the extent and sublime magnificence of the view. The mountains lay all around them, clothed with a velvet-like covering of the softest green, and between them lay an endless number and variety of lakes and rivers—all sleeping apparently in the sun—and green fields, and pretty villages, and charming glens, in endless variety.

After remaining upon the mountain for about fifteen minutes, they all set out upon their return. They of course came down the path very easily, and getting into the dog-cart, when they reached the foot of the descent, they were driven very rapidly back to the inn.

CHAPTER XII.

THE CALEDONIAN CANAL.

The route of the steamer from the foot of Ben Nevis to Inverness, lies along a remarkable chain of lakes, that occupy a long and narrow valley extending through the very heart of Scotland, in a direction from southwest to northeast, and reaching from the base of Ben Nevis to Inverness. The line of these lakes is easily to be seen upon the map. In a state of nature the lakes were connected by rapid streams flowing from the center lake, which is the highest, down through the others each way to the sea. But though the lakes themselves were navigable, the streams were not. Many years ago, however, as has already been intimated, deep channels were cut along these streams, and locks made wherever there was an ascent or descent, so as to form a navigable communication through the whole distance, which received the name of the Caledonian canal.

Mrs. Morelle and her party, remained a day or two at the foot of Ben Nevis, taking little excursions in the environs, and exploring for a few miles, in various directions, the glens which open around the mountain. On the morning of the third day, they took the steamer again, at a place called Banavie, where there was a large and beautiful hotel, standing almost by itself in a wild and beautiful place, and surrounded by gardens and ornamental grounds A great many of the best inns and hotels in Scotland, stand thus in secluded places, entirely apart from the towns, being intended altogether for the accommodation of tourists journeying for pleasure, and being placed accordingly in the localities where it is supposed to be most convenient or most agreeable for such travellers to stop.

By having rested from the steamer two days, the children were well prepared to return to it again, and they had a delightful passage along the canal. Sometimes they found themselves sailing in a very narrow channel which had been excavated artificially, to connect one lake with another. Next they would come to a chain of locks, by means of which the steamer was to be raised up, or let down, from one level to another; and while the lockmen were engaged in this operation, which always required some time, the passengers would step out upon the embankment, and ramble about the neighborhood, or walk on to the next lock, with a view of getting on board again when the steamer came to it. Then at length, suddenly the steamer would emerge from the narrow and artificial channel into one of the lakes, and would glide swiftly on from one end of it to the other, between the lofty ranges of mountains which bordered it on either hand.

In all cases, the course of the steamer was so near to the shore, that all the features of the scenery could be very distinctly seen, and it was an endless source of amusement to the children to watch the changes which were continually taking place, and to explore every hidden recess of the landscape, and examine every detail with the glass. They saw the sheep feeding on the mountain sides, watched by the shepherd and his dog, and the cottages, with Highland children, dressed in the kilt, playing at the doors, and now and then an elegant travelling carriage moving along the road at the margin of the water.

There were a great many mists and clouds floating over the mountain tops, and these increased toward the middle of the day. For a time the effect of these clouds was only to add an additional feature of grandeur to the scenery, by the magnificent forms which the stupendous masses of vapor assumed on the summits of the mountain chains, and the mysterious and solemn gloom which they seemed to impart to the deep valleys, by hanging over them in heavy folds, like those of a curtain, and diffusing through the recesses which they half concealed, a dark and impenetrable gloom. Florence said that she could not decide whether she liked the mountains best when full in view, or when half covered with clouds.

"Nor I," said Grimkie. "Only it is raining from some of those clouds. All I am afraid of is, that one of them may come and rain upon us."

Grimkie's fears were destined to be realized. In a short time it began to rain upon the deck of the steamer. Some of the passengers, especially the ladies, hastily gathering up their maps, and guide books, and travelling bags, went below. Others drew themselves into as compact a mass as possible, and spreading an umbrella over their heads, kept their seats. Some gentlemen put on India rubber coats, which they seemed to have ready at hand, and went on walking up and down the deck just as before. One of the men belonging on board the steamer came up from below, and took up all the cushions which were not in use, and carried them down. He also gathered together all books, bags, shawls and other such things as any of the passengers had left exposed, and putting them upon the end of a seat he covered them with a tarpaulin. He also gathered together all the camp-stools which were not in use, and put them under cover.

Mrs. Morelle went below as soon as the first drops of the shower began to fall, leaving the children to remain if they chose. Grimkie found a place which was in a good degree sheltered from the wind and rain, and there, placing Florence upon one camp-stool in the middle, and John upon another at the side of her, while he took his place upon the other side, and then after spreading a large travelling shawl, or rug as the English call it, over their knees, and tucking it in well all around, he opened his umbrella, which was very large, and looking out from under it at the shower, he said,

"Now let it rain."

For some time the children seemed to enjoy the scene and the novelty of their situation, but before long they began to get tired, and at length they determined to avail themselves of the first opportunity, when the rain should slacken a little, to go below.

"I have got something for us to do there,"

said Grimkie. "We shall get the benefit of Mr. Twig's advice."

"Who is Mr. Twig?" asked Florence.

"He is the gentleman on board the steamer," replied Grimkie, "that told me about travelling in Scotland. He said that one of the most important things, was to provide plenty of employment for rainy days. It rained, he said, in Scotland about half the time."

"Oh, Grimkie!" exclaimed John.

"Among the Highlands, he meant," said Grimkie. "He said that the Gulf of Mexico, the Atlantic Ocean, and the Highlands and islands of Scotland formed one great distilling appartus. The Gulf of Mexico was the boiler, and the mountains in Scotland the condenser.

"But come," added Grimkie, interrupting himself, "it does not rain much just this moment. Let us go below."

So they rose from their seats, and taking every thing with them they hurried along the deck to the companion-way and went below.

They found a very pretty cabin, handsomely carpeted, with four long tables in it, two on each side, and cushioned seats behind them. There was also a row of small windows, with sliding sashes, above, from which they could look out over the water. Groups of passengers were sitting here and there at the tables. Some were looking over their maps and guide books, and others were lounging on the seats with a listless air, as if they had had no one to forewarn them, as Mr. Twig had done for Grimkie, of the necessity of providing work for rainy days.

Grimkie found seats for his party at one of the tables. He placed his aunt and Florence at the back side of it, upon one of the cushioned seats, and set camp-stools for himself and John in front. He then went for his knapsack.

This knapsack Grimkie always kept with him in travelling. He bought it in Liverpool. It was made of morocco, of a bronze-green color, and was provided with a strap which was arranged in such a way that the knapsack could be suspended from the shoulder, or carried in the hand like a bag. In it Grimkie carried his portfolio, his writing apparatus, Mrs. Morelle's opera-glass, the map, the guide book, and other such things as it was necessary to have always at hand.

When he had brought the knapsack he laid it down upon the table, and as soon as he had taken his seat, he opened it and took out his portfolio, containing Florence's flowers.

"Ah!" said Florence, "here are my flowers."

Grimkie had collected a large number of delicate Alpine flowers, for Florence, during their ascent of Ben Nevis, and had put them all carefully between the leaves of the blotting paper book, which he had made for her. On the evening of the same day, on his return from the mountain, he had looked over all these flowers and rearranged them. In doing this, he cut off with the point of a pair of scissors, all the superfluous parts, smoothed out the little leaves, bent the stems into graceful forms, and put them into fresh places between the leaves. When he had done all this, he placed the book under a small piece of board which he found in the yard of the hotel, and put the whole beneath one of the legs of the bedstead in his room, which of course subjected the book, and the plants between the leaves of it, to a heavy pressure.

The next morning, when the party were about to leave the hotel, Grimkie took out the book, and after winding a long tape round it a great many times, and tying the ends, he crowded some wedges in on both sides, between the tape and book covers. This produced a pressure upon the plants which, though not so great as before, was sufficient at this stage of the process.

It was this book, thus tied up and wedged, that Grimkie now took out from his knapsack.

"That's a nice way to press the flowers," said Florence.

"Yes," replied Grimkie, "only the sides of the book are not stiff enough to wedge against. I ought to have two thin pieces of board, just the size of the book covers, to put upon them, one on each side."

Grimkie opened the book and looked at the flowers. They were pressed very nicely, and the colors of the flowers were well preserved. He also took out from his knapsack some sheets of white note paper, which he proceeded to fold into quarters and then to cut them open at the foldings with a knife, so as to make a number of little sheets of paper of about the size and shape of visiting cards, each one, however, having, like the original sheet of note paper, two leaves. He gave these to Florence as fast as he made them, that she might trim the edges with her scissors. These sheets were to gum the little flowers upon.

He also took from his knapsack, a small bottle of gum arabic. This bottle was very small, being not much bigger than a large thimble, and it was very strong, so as not to be in any danger of breaking, by being carried in a knapsack.

Grimkie took out the cork from this bottle, and then proceeded to select from his stock of flowers, two or three of different kinds, such as could be arranged together prettily in the form of a bouquet. These he proceeded to gum upon one of his little sheets of paper. He would take out a very small quantity of the dissolved gum arabic,—which was very thick,—being of about the consistence of honey, and then touch a very little of it, delicately at different points on the under side of the flower. Then he would lay down the flower upon the inside page of one of his little sheets of note paper, taking care to place it in exactly the position in which he meant it to lie.

Presently Florence and John after seeing how Grimkie managed the work, undertook it themselves, each selecting flowers from among those which had been pressed, and gumming them upon the paper. In this manner, in the course of half an hour, quite a number of very pretty specimens were prepared.

The flowers were in all cases gummed upon what may be called the third page of the little sheet of note paper: that is, upon the right hand page of the second leaf, on the inside. The first leaf then, when laid down, covered and protected the flower.

"When we stop at the next hotel," said Grimkie, "we will write upon these little sheets what the flowers are, and where they come from, and then put them all up for you Florence in a package, and so when you get back to America you can distribute them among your friends."

Just at this time the attention of the whole party was suddenly attracted to a gleam of sunshine, which came in through one of the windows and fell upon the floor. John immediately abandoned every thing and hurried away to go on deck. Grimkie after putting all his apparatus carefully away in his knapsack, followed him, saying to his aunt and Florence that he would come back in a moment and tell them whether it was dry enough for them to come up too.

In a few minutes Grimkie came down and said that the steamer was going to stop pretty soon in a certain place on the border of the lake, in order to allow the passengers to go on shore to see a waterfall.

"To see a waterfall!" exclaimed Mrs. Morelle. "I never heard of such a thing as a steamer's stopping for the passengers to see a waterfall. You don't mean that she is going to wait for us."

"Yes, Auntie," said Grimkie. "That is it. She is going to wait here while we go up and see it, and then come back. It is only a little way."

"Let us go, then, by all means," said Mrs. Morelle.

Mrs. Morelle decided to go at once, without stopping to make any inquiries. Cases of this kind often occur in which an experienced traveller is safe in taking things upon trust, without making inquiries. Mrs. Morelle saw at a glance that a steamer would not stop for such a purpose unless the fall was really remarkable, and well worthy the attention of the tourists on board, nor without having proper arrangements made, in respect to guides, paths, and all other necessary facilities for going to and from the place. So when, on ascending to the deck, she found the ladies and gentlemen generally preparing to go on shore, she determined at once to join them, especially as it was plain that there was no time for obtaining any information, as the steamer was now close to the pier.

It was a small pier, projecting out a little way from the shore, in a very wild and solitary place.

The mountain-side rose quite abruptly from the surface of the water, half covered with forests, and there was no town, nor even any house in sight. There was nothing but a small building at the end of the pier near which a kind of cab, or short omnibus without any covering over it, was standing.

The steamer was soon made fast and the passengers went on shore. Most of them began at once to walk up a road which was seen ascending in a diagonal manner through the trees. Some of the ladies were getting into the cab.

"Auntie," said Grimkie. "They are going to ride up. You had better ride too."

"How far is it?" asked Mrs. Morelle.

"I don't know at all," said Grimkie. "Only it must be far enough to ride, or else they would not have a carriage."

This reasoning seemed very conclusive, but Mrs. Morelle turned to a gentleman who was walking near her with a lady upon his arm, and asked him if he knew how far it was to the fall.

"No madam," said he with a smile, "we don't know any thing about it. We are only following the multitude."

Mrs. Morelle might perhaps have asked half or two thirds of the whole company without receiving any other answer than this.

"I think you had better ride, Auntie," said Grimkie. "That will be the safest way."

Mrs. Morelle acceded to this proposal and Grimkie helped her into the cab, and then he followed Florence and John up the road.

The road was a most excellent one. It was not very wide, but it was perfectly made, and the borders of it on each side were finished as nicely as if it had been a walk in a gentleman's private grounds. The land was very steep, both above and below it, and the slopes were covered with forest trees. The road ascended in a zigzag direction, in long reaches, though the children soon came to places where there were short cuts by a foot-path from one angle of the road to another, which they found that most of the people who were walking took, and so they took them too.

They went on in this way for nearly half an hour, ascending all the time, and at length they seemed to have left the carriage road altogether. At last, however, they came out into it again at a place where they could hear the roar of the waterfall in a deep ravine below them. The tourists seemed to find out by some sort of instinct that this was the place where the carriage was to come, and so those who had ladies in the carriage stopped here, to wait for the carriage to come up, while the others began to go down a steep zigzag path which led into the ravine.

"We will wait here," said Grimkie, "until Auntie comes."

It was not long before the carriage came, and all the ladies who had rode up in it got out. They then all began to go down the zigzag path into the ravine. The scenery in the chasm was grand beyond description. The path, as it changed its direction at the different turns, brought continually new portions of the vast chasm into view, and revealed awful depths which it made one dizzy to look down into. At the same time the thundering of the cataract, reverberating from the rocky precipices which formed the sides of the chasm filled the air with a deafening sound.

At length the path came to an end on a pinnacle of rock, where there was room for only one or two to stand at a time, and where the fall itself was in full view. It was an immense torrent coming down through a vast fissure in the rocks above, and falling with the noise of thunder, eighty or ninety feet, into an awful abyss below.

It was fearful to stand upon the dizzy pinnacle where the path terminated, and attempt to look down into the gulf half hidden by mist and spray into which the cataract descended. Only one or two could stand there at a time, and the visitors were consequently obliged to take turns. Mrs. Morelle allowed the children to go, one at a time, while she held them nervously to prevent their falling, and right glad she was when they all had seen it and she could go away.

The company lingered a little while at the different turns of the path to look down into the chasm. It was of a very irregular form, and it presented new and striking aspects at every new point of view. It was very impressive to survey the precipitous rocks, the trees clinging to the crevices on the sides, and the foaming torrents forcing their way furiously through the devious and rocky channels at an immense depth below.

After a time all the passengers had ascended to the place where the carriage had been left. The ladies who had rode up took their places in it again, and began to descend the hill by the road, while the rest of the party went down more rapidly by the short cuts which the footpath followed.

Grimkie waited at the bottom until the carriage came down, and then, after helping his aunt to descend, and paying the driver of the carriage the shilling fare, they all went together again on board the steamer.

The name of this cataract is the Fall of Foyers. It is on the shore of Loch Ness, the last of the lakes which lie on the line of the Caledonian canal; and not many hours from the time of resuming the voyage, after visiting the fall, the steamer arrived at its destination at Inverness.

As the party went into the town from the place of debarkation, they all gazed about them with great curiosity and interest. They saw the river Ness flowing rapidly along between green and beautiful banks, and a long and massive stone bridge leading across it, and a grand looking castle on the brow of a hill bordering the town overlooking the river, and a compact mass of grey stone houses, ancient and venerable in appearance, but snug, tidy, and all in excellent order. Nothing was imperfect or unfinished. There was no building going on, nor any improvements of any kind in progress. Florence said it looked as if the town had been completed fifty years before, and that thenceforth nothing had been done, and nothing was ever to be done but to keep everything in it in the nicest order.

There were the neatest and prettiest little graveled roads extending along the banks of the river on either side, which promised to be charming walks, and ornamented grounds here and there which seemed to be open to the public, and high craggy summits of hills seen in the environs that Grimkie said he must ascend. On the whole the aspect of the town and of its environs was charming. But the party could only get occasional glimpses of the view, for they were driven along rapidly in their carriage, and at length stopped in the middle of a street, at the door of a very snug, compact, and quiet-looking hotel, called the Union Hotel. Grimkie had chosen it from its name, partly on account of the American associations connected with that word, and partly for the sake of variety. The other principal hotel in the town was the Caledonian; and as it was the Caledonian canal on which they had been travelling all day, Grimkie said it would make an agreeable change, he thought, to take some other name for the hotel.

After the party became settled at the hotel, John, on reflecting upon the name, wondered at first that one of so peculiarly American a meaning should be given to an inn in so remote a part of Scotland. He concluded that it must have been given out of compliment to the Americans, in hopes of attracting their custom; just as he had seen "New York Hotel" at Glasgow. He at length ventured to ask a respectable looking gentleman who was standing at the door what the name denoted. The gentleman answered him as follows, in broad Scotch:

"It is joost to commemorate the union of the two kingdoms of England and Scotland," said he. "Ye ken that in former days they were separate altogether, but at length by marriages and intermarriages atween the twa royal hooses, they baith descended to the same heir, who was James Sixth of Scotland and First of England. But still the twa kingdoms were separate, each with its own parliament and its own laws, although they were ruled over by one and the same king. This was found in the end not to be convenient, and so finally an act of union was passed by which the twa realms themselves were moulded and merged into ane, with ane only parliament at London to make laws for the whole. This was the famous union, and ye will larn all aboot it, when ye get a little older and study Scottish history."

On hearing this, John went in and told Grimkie that he had missed it in coming to that hotel, for the union of it was not the American Union at all.

CHAPTER XIII.

THE VITRIFIED FORT.

The party arrived at the hotel about the middle of the afternoon. After getting somewhat settled in their rooms, Grimkie ordered dinner at five o'clock, and then, while Mrs. Morelle and Florence were occupied in their chamber, he and John went out to take a walk.

They spent their time during their walk in rambling along the principal streets of the town, occupying themselves with looking at the curious dresses of the people, hearing the little children talk broad Scotch in their play, and examining the objects displayed in the shop windows. Many of these objects were very curious, especially the bracelets, and pins, and brooches, made of Scotch pebbles, many of which were of the most singular forms, being made after the fashion of the different clans of Highlanders, as they wore them in ancient times.

"You may depend upon it my mother will buy some of these pins," said John.

There were also a number of curious articles

made of wood painted in tartan, according to the fashion of the different clans, such as boxes, card-cases, needle-books, pen-holders, paper-folders, and many other such things.

When the time drew near which had been appointed for dinner, the boys went home, and very soon after they arrived the dinner was brought in. While they were at table, Grimkie asked his aunt, whether she was not glad, so far, that she had come.

"Yes," said she, "very glad indeed. We have had a delightful voyage among the mountains and lakes, but I feel tired and I have a great idea of going into lodgings here for a week to rest and recruit."

"Oh, mother!" exclaimed Florence, "we have not had anything to tire us. We have had nothing to do but to sit quietly on the deck of the steamer, and look at the scenery."

"It is not my body that is tired," said Mrs. Morelle, "but my mind. I have been continually wondering and admiring for four or five days, and I am tired of wondering and admiring. I want to be quiet a little while, to rest my mind, and get ready to begin again. And the best way to do that is to go into lodgings. I see lodgings to let, on several of the houses along the street."

The English system in respect to accommodations for strangers at private houses, as well as that of the hotels, is entirely different from the usage which prevails in America. Instead of boarding houses, they have what is called lodging houses. In one of these houses, the party travelling, if they wish to remain some days in any place, and to spend the time in a more quiet and domestic way than by remaining at a hotel, take apartments and keep house, precisely as if they were in their own home. After looking at the different rooms, and hearing the prices of each, they select as many as they require, and take possession of them, paying so much a day for them. The price which they pay for the rooms, includes the necessary service, and the *cooking* of the food, but not the purchase of it. The lodger may either purchase the food for himself, going to the market for it every day, just as if he were keeping house at home, or he may request the landlady to purchase it for him. In case he adopts the latter plan, the landlady keeps an account of what she expends, and brings him in the bill every morning.

In a word, at an English lodging house a lady stopping to rest for a week, finds herself keeping house, just as if she were at home, with an experienced, capable, and motherly woman to act as her housekeeper, and to do every thing that she requires. She can arrange the expenses too just as she pleases, for every thing except the price of the rooms, which is agreed upon beforehand, is under her immediate control.

English ladies when they take lodgings in this way, usually go out themselves to the grocers and to the markets, to purchase their provisions and supplies—but American ladies, not being so well acquainted with English marketing, usually give the landlady a memorandum in the morning of what they would like during the day, and the landlady then makes the purchases.

In addition to the domestic quiet and repose which the traveller obtains by taking lodgings, when he wishes to remain in any town for several days, there is a great advantage in the arrangement, in point of economy. The expense is only from one-third to one-half, for the same rooms and style of living, at the lodging-houses of what it costs at the hotels.

Mrs. Morelle had often experienced the advantage of stopping occasionally for a week, and going into lodgings, when she had been travelling in Europe before. But the children knew nothing about the system. They were, however, always ready for any new plan which was proposed, and in coming into Inverness they had seen so much to attract their attention that they were perfectly willing to remain there a week. So it was determined that they should remain at the hotel that night, and the next morning go and look out for lodgings.

But the next morning Mrs. Morelle found herself so well rested, by a good night's sleep that she began to feel inclined to go on.

"The next portion of our journey is by the stage-coach, Grimkie, is it not?" said she.

Grimkie said that it was. They were to go by a circuitous route, following the indentations of the shore to Wick, and there to wait for the Edinburgh steamer.

"And I believe," said Grimkie, "that the steamer only goes once a week, and it touches at Wick every Friday night, at midnight."

"At midnight," repeated Mrs. Morelle.

"Yes, Auntie," said Grimkie, "but that will not make any difference. It will be as light as day."

"That will be funny," said John.

"Let us send for Boots," said Mrs. Morelle, "and ascertain exactly how it is."

So Grimkie rang the bell and asked the waiter to send up Boots, and when he came they obtained from him all the necessary information. He said that the coach left Inverness every evening at eight o'clock—that it travelled all night—that about two o'clock it crossed a wide ferry called the Mickle Ferry—a mile wide—that it arrived at Wick about ten o'clock on the following day, and that the steamer would arrive from Edinburgh in the course of Friday night, and they would have to go on board early on Saturday morning.

The children were all very much pleased to learn that they were to ride in the stage-coach all night, and even Mrs. Morelle did not object to it on the whole. She concluded, however, not to remain at Inverness, as she had at first intended, but to go directly on as far as Wick. It was on Wednesday, when the party arrived at Inverness, and in order to be in time for the steamer of that week, it would be necessary to leave that very evening, and this she determined to do.

"And then," said she, "when we arrive at Wick, in case the weather is favorable we will go on board the steamer and accomplish our voyage. If it is not favorable then we can go into lodgings and spend our week there."

"Yes, Auntie," said Grimkie, "John and I will like that very much, for then we can see the fishing boats go out and come in. Wick is the greatest place in the world for the herring fishery.

The guide book says there are fifteen hundred large fishing boats that belong there."

The plan being thus arranged, Grimkie and John went to the coach to "book" as they called it, for Wick. They were very desirous, of taking outside seats for themselves, and inside seats, which are much dearer, for the two ladies; but Mrs. Morelle was afraid to have the boys sit outside all night, for fear that they might get asleep and fall off. So she requested them to take the four inside seats for the party, promising that if there was room outside, and the coachman had no objection, they should ride there a part of the time.

Accordingly, Grimkie went to the coach office, and took all the four inside seats and paid the fare. The clerk said that the travellers must be at the office, with their luggage at a quarter before eight.

When the two boys returned to the hotel, they found a large open carriage before the door, and Mrs. Morelle and Florence preparing to take a drive around the environs of Inverness to see the scenery. Mrs. Morelle invited the two boys to join the party, which invitation they were of course very ready to accept. Grimkie proposed, too that, in the course of the ride the carriage should stop at the foot of Craig Phadric, and that they should all go up and see the remains of a vitrified fort that he said existed there.

In furtherance of this suggestion, he opened one of his books and read an account of the vitrified forts.

These forts are objects of great curiosity to tourists and antiquarians. They exist in various parts of the country, and are so ancient that not only all records, but even all traditions of their origin is lost. They are referred to in the very earliest accounts of the country that exist, as ruins and remains exhibiting the same appearance then as they now present, and enveloped in the same mystery in respect to their origin.

There are a great many of these old forts in different parts of the country, and the thing which chiefly characterizes them, and the one from which they derive their name, is that the stones of which the walls are composed instead of being cemented together by mortar, are fused, or vitrified, as if by the action of great heat, into one continuous mass. It is not possible to ascertain the exact nature of this vitrification, for the walls of these forts have nearly disappeared, leaving only long ridges of ruins, covered in the main with earth, and turfed over ; and in many cases immense trees are growing upon them. Portions of the old walls, however, appear here and there above the ground, and by a little digging they may be uncovered at any point along the line, when the stones, melted together, are brought to view.

A great many different suppositions have been advanced by antiquarians to account for the origin of these works. Some suppose that they were erected in times before the use of cement was known, and that the people of those days resorted to this mode of consolidating their masonry, not knowing any other. They think that they laid up the wall first in the usual way, selecting such stones as would vitrify by heat, and then built immense fires against them, and kept up the heat by replenishing the fires continually until the effect was produced.

It has been supposed that in order to concentrate the heat, and economize fuel, the builders were accustomed to build a second wall outside the first, and very near it, leaving only interval enough for the fuel to be laid in.

It must be confessed, however, that some persons who have examined these remains, have suggested that perhaps the vitrification was not produced purposely at all, but was an accidental effect, resulting from the building of great beacon fires on the hills where the forts stand, perhaps long after the forts themselves fell to ruin.

It is a fact that the vitrified forts are generally situated on commanding elevations. It is also a well-known fact that in ancient times it was the universal custom, in all this region, to extend the alarm through the country in case of war, by immense beacon fires built upon the hills; and it has been suggested accordingly, that it might have been in some accidental way like this, and not by any special design and process of art, that the vitrification was produced.

Grimkie had read accounts of these forts in the different books that he had consulted, and was very desirous of visiting one of them. He was influenced in this desire, not only by a wish to see the fort, but he also wished to procure a specimen of the stones fused together to carry home, and add to the museum at the Chateau. And thus it was that he proposed to his aunt, when they were getting into the carriage to go and take their ride, that they should drive first to the foot of Craig Phadric, and so go up and see the fort.

"How high is Craig Phadric?" asked Mrs. Morelle. "Is it as high as Ben Nevis?"

"Oh no, Auntie," replied Grimkie. "It is only two or three hundred feet high."

"Because I don't feel quite able to undertake a second Ben Nevis just yet," said Mrs. Morelle.

"It will be nothing like Ben Nevis, Auntie," said Grimkie. "They never would make a fortification on such a mountain as that. Besides you will not be obliged to go any farther than you like. If we find it too steep, or too high, we can turn back again at any time."

"Ah!" replied Mrs. Morelle, laughing, "that is the way you got me up to the top of Ben Nevis, by pretending that I could turn about whenever I pleased."

"Oh no, Auntie! I did not *pretend*," said Grimkie. "You really *could* turn about whenever you pleased. I think I was very honest about it. Though I confess I hoped all the time that you would get to the top."

"Yes," said Mrs. Morelle, "you were honest, and I am very glad that you managed as you did, and that it ended in my going to the top of the mountain. And we will go to Craig Phadric now. I won't promise to go up, but on the way you shall tell us about the vitrified fort, as you call it, that we are to see there."

So they all got into the carriage, and directed the coachman to drive to the foot of the Craig Phadric.

On the way Grimkie gave his aunt an account of the particulars in respect to vitrified forts, which have been stated above. His aunt was very much interested in what he said, having never heard of the vitrified forts before. She became still more interested in the idea of making the ascent, when she came to see the hill itself, which was in full view as the carriage crossed the bridge. It was a high hill, well wooded except upon one side, where the rocks were exposed to view, naked and precipitous.

After ascending by a winding road for some time, the coachman stopped the horses near a small farm house, close under the hill, and on getting down from the carriage the party saw a small path leading through the woods up the ascent. They took this path and after following it for about ten minutes through various meanderings and windings they found themselves upon the summit.

Here the remains of the fort lay before them, though they were all somewhat disappointed in the appearance of them. They had expected to see some solid walls with the outside surface of them fused into a black and glass-like slag. Instead of this, however, there were only long embankments of earth, forming an immense parallelogram which occupied the whole top of the hill. These embankments as well as various detached mounds which were connected with them in various places in the form of outworks, were almost entirely grassed over, and from the firm and compact turf which enveloped them, immense trees were growing everywhere. Indeed, the whole of the ground occupied by the fort was covered with a forest of ancient and venerable-looking trees, the effect of which was to impart an air of strange solitude and solemnity to the scene, which made it extremely impressive. Mrs. Morelle said that though she was a little disappointed in what she saw, she was far more than repaid by what she *felt*, in walking over the ruins, or rather the remains, and that she would not on any account have failed of visiting the spot.

After rambling about for some time, Grimkie at length found several places where portions of the old wall were exposed to view, and though they were mere shapeless masses of stones that he thus found, they appeared to be fused together by heat. After pounding among them for a while he succeeded in obtaining several good specimens of the curious conglomerate, to carry with him to America. He selected also a very pretty specimen, the smallest that he could find, for Florence, and others similar to it for Mrs. Morelle and John.

After satisfying themselves with an examination of the fort, Grimkie led the way out of the wood toward the brow of the precipice, which formed the side of the hill next the town. Here they enjoyed a magnificent prospect of the whole valley, with the river Ness flowing through the center of it, the bridge over it, leading into the town, the town itself, and the castle by its side. Florence thought that this view was far more worth seeing than the fort.

"So do I," said John. "In fact I don't think much of the fort. I've seen just such banks as those on the Heights of Dorchester once, when I was in Boston."

"True," said his mother, "only those were not a hundred years old, and these are probably two thousand."

"That does not make any difference in the looks of them," replied John.

"No," said his mother, "but it makes some difference in the *feelings* with which we regard them."

"It does not make much difference in mine," said John.

Just then John saw something alive running off through the woods.

"It is a rabbit," said he, and he darted off at full speed, taking aim at the same time with his specimen of the vitrification. Grimkie called him to come back, but before he had time to obey the stone flew from his hand through the air, and at last struck the trunk of a tree very near where the rabbit had disappeared, and rebounded from it with great force.

"Johnnie!" said Grimkie, speaking in a very stern voice. "It is very lucky for you that you did not hit that rabbit."

"Why so?" asked John.

"If you had hit him and killed him, you would have been a poacher. Any body that kills any kind of game in this country, unless the owner of the land gives him leave, is a poacher. Did not you ever read the story of Black Giles the Poacher?"

"Yes," said John; "but he did things a great deal worse than killing rabbits out in the woods. I tell you these rabbits don't belong to any body. I don't believe the *land* here belongs to any body. It is *wild* land."

"We should find that it belonged to some body," replied Grimkie, "if people should catch us killing rabbits here."

John had a sort of instinctive feeling that Grimkie was right, but he consoled himself for his discomforture in the argument by saying that at any rate he came within one of hitting the rabbit.

The subject here dropped, as the reporters in

Parliament say, and the whole party returned down the hill.

"Now, Auntie," said Grimkie, as they rode back to the hotel, "the clerk said we must be at the stage office at a quarter before eight. Would you like to ride there?"

"If it is not far," said his aunt, "we can walk just as well, and so we shall see more of the town."

"Yes," said Grimkie, "I should like that, and Mr. Boots will carry our luggage for us."

CHAPTER XIV.

NIGHT RIDE BY DAYLIGHT.

A LITTLE before eight o'clock that evening, the whole party proceeded on foot from the hotel to the stage office. The porter of the hotel went with them, taking the trunk and some smaller parcels. The coach soon came out in front of the office, the trunk and the parcels were put upon the roof. Mrs. Morelle and Florence took their places inside, while Grimkie and John mounted to the top, and established themselves upon a long cushioned seat, which extended from one side of the coach to the other, directly behind the coachman.

Instead of a rack behind, as in American stage-coaches, there was a sort of box, with a door opening into it, for the mail bags, and seats above, over the back part of the coach. One of these seats is occupied by the man who has care of the mails, and who is called the guard. The other seats are for such passengers as choose to ride there. Grimkie and John, however, chose

NIGHT RIDE BY DAYLIGHT. 189

to ride on the forward seat, so that they could see before them as they rode along.

The coach drove first through the village and stopped at the postoffice to take the mails, where quite a little crowd of men and boys assembled to witness the setting off. The horses were soon in motion again, the coachman cracking his whip with a very smart air, as the wheels ran rapidly over the pavement. From their elevated seat, Grimkie and John could look down with great advantage upon every thing around them. They soon came to the end of the pavement, and then the horses trotted and cantered swiftly along over a hard and smooth road, across the canal by a beautiful bridge, and then on among green fields, through turnpike gates, and along the walls of gardens, and parks, and pleasure-grounds, while pretty cottages, and porters' lodges, and green hedges, and milestones, and peasant girls, going or returning from milking, and a thousand other such objects as mark the rural scenery of Scotland in a summer evening, glided by them in rapid succession.

In the distance all around them lofty mountains were seen, the summits of some of them covered with snow, and the sun still high in the sky in the northwest, though half concealed by golden clouds, promised to accompany and cheer them on their journey for a long time.

"It is after eight o'clock," said Grimkie, "and see how high the sun is!"

"Very high," said John. "I don't believe the sun will set before ten o'clock."

"Yes, the sun sets here a little after nine," said Grimkie.

"How do you know?" asked John.

"I looked in a Glasgow almanac," replied Grimkie. "The sun sets in Glasgow one or two minutes after nine to night, and here it must be some minutes later, for we are two or three degrees farther north."

"I don't see why that is any reason," said John.

"Oh that is very plain," rejoined Grimkie. "Don't you see that we are going round over the curvature of the earth toward the north?"

As he said this, Grimkie made a gesture with his hand, pushing it out before him in a manner to denote a motion in advance over the curved surface of a ball.

"Yes," said John.

"And don't you see that the sun is going down over the roundness of the earth in the same direction?"

"Yes," said John, "almost in the north—in the north*west*."

"Then don't you perceive," added Grimkie, "that the farther we go, on the same course that he is going, the longer we can see him?"

"Ah yes," said John. "And that is the reason why we shall see the sun longer here to-night than they will in Glasgow."

"Exactly," said Grimkie.

In the meantime the horses, having been now trotting and galloping for about an hour over the hard and smooth road, were brought up by the coachman somewhat suddenly at the door of an inn in a small village, in order to be changed. The coachman descended from his seat, the post-boys led out the fresh horses from the stable of the inn, and the guard took the mail bags which were to be left at that place out of his box, and threw them down into the road.

Grimkie availed himself of this opportunity to inquire after the welfare of his aunt and cousin. He leaned over as far as he could on one side, toward the coach window below, and called out:

"Auntie, are you getting along pretty well?"

Immediately Florence's head appeared at the window.

"Grimkie," said she, "where are we?"

"We have stopped to change horses," said Grimkie.

"Already?" said Florence.

"Yes," said Grimkie. "When the horses go so fast they have to be changed very often. Have you got a good seat?"

"An excellent seat," said Florence. "I have got a window all to myself."

"And can you see the country?" asked Grimkie.

"Oh, yes!" said Florence, "I can see it beautifully, I have got one window and mother has got the other."

"And mother says," she added, after turning her head a moment, "that you and Johnnie must be careful not to fall off."

"There is no danger, tell her," replied Grimkie. "We have good safe seats, with an iron railing at the two ends to keep us in."

By this time the fresh horses were put in, and the coachman having mounted to his place again, the coach was soon rolling on along the road, faster even than before.

Soon after this the sun went down, but the clouds which he left behind him in the western sky, were for a time almost as bright as he himself had been, so that at half past nine there seemed to be no sensible diminution of the light of day. The track of the sun too, in going down, was so oblique to the horizon, that even at half-past ten his distance below it was very small, and Grimkie and John could see the country all about them, and the time by their watches, and the places through which they were passing, just as well almost as ever.

From half-past ten to eleven there was still very little change. The children were all playing in the streets of the villages that they passed, and groups of men and boys had collected at the doors of the inns where they stopped, as they would have done at half-past seven or eight o'clock in a summer evening in America. Even the hens did not seem to know that it was night, for they were rambling about, and scratching at every unusual appearance on the grounds, as briskly as in any part of the day.

"I don't see how the children know when to go to bed," said John.

"Or the hens either," said Grimkie. "A Connecticut rooster I should think would be greatly mystified here. He would not lead his hens off to roost until he saw it growing dark,—and then if he began to crow again as soon as he saw any light, he would not give them any time to sleep at all."

After eleven o'clock the boys found that at each succeeding village or hamlet that they came to fewer and fewer people appeared, until at length at twelve, and between twelve and one, the country seemed deserted, and yet the light continued. It was a strange thing, the boys thought, to drive into a village in broad daylight, and to find the streets silent and solitary, and without a person being visible at any door or window; and still more sometimes, when they stopped to change horses, to see that the coachman was obliged to knock upon the stable-door to wake the ostlers up, while by the aspect of the whole scene around, there was nothing that betokened night.

It was not much after midnight when the coach arrived at the Mickle Ferry. The Mickle Ferry means the *great* ferry. It is so called to distinguish it from another smaller one in the neighborhood called the Little Ferry. The Mickle Ferry passes across a narrow part of the Dornoch Firth, as may be seen by the map. The firth is a mile or two wide, at the ferry, and is crossed in a large flat-bottomed sail-boat, sufficient to convey the passengers and their luggage in perfect safety,—but not large enough for the coach.

The coach was accordingly to be left on the hither side of the ferry, another being provided on the farther side, to receive the passengers at the landing and take them on.

The company in the coach, accordingly, on

CROSSING THE MICKLE FERRY.

arriving at the margin of the water, descended from the coach and walked down the sloping pier to the boat, and went on board. Mrs. Morelle had felt some apprehension at the idea of crossing a wide ferry in an open boat at midnight, but she found, on arriving at the spot, that there was no occasion for alarm. The boat was very wide, and appeared very steady ; and as to midnight,—it might as well have been eight o'clock of a bright summer evening at home. It is true that the sun was entirely below the horizon, but the whole northern sky was brightly illuminated by his beams, and so light was it upon the water, that Grimkie said that if he had a newspaper, he would amuse them during the passage by reading the news.

The boat was wafted very rapidly, but yet with a very smooth and gentle motion, across the water. The passengers landed on the farther side, and the luggage was taken out, and in a few minutes the new coach was seen coming rapidly down the road toward the landing place in order to receive the travellers and convey them onward.

Mrs. Morelle now proposed that the two boys should get inside, but they were extremely desirous to continue upon the top, and as the coachman assured Mrs. Morelle that the seat was perfectly safe for them, even if they should fall asleep, she consented that they should remain. Besides it was now after one o'clock, and it was growing lighter quite fast. In a little more than an hour, as Grimkie calculated, it would be nearly sunrise.

The country now became very picturesque and wild, the sea being brought continually into full view as the horses trotted swiftly round the curves of the road, following the undulations of the coast. At one place it descended by a winding and zigzag way into an immense ravine a mile or two across. The sides of the ravine were covered with forest, and there was a river and a village at the bottom of it.

After traversing this ravine, the road followed the line of the coast, passing by many great castles, and presenting here and there magnificent views of the sea. Mrs. Morelle and Florence lost some of these views, for they fell asleep; and even John, upon the top, nodded several times, though he insisted, whenever Grimkie asked him about it, that he was not in the least sleepy.

At length, toward noon of Friday, the coach arrived safely at Wick.

The passengers were all very glad to reach the termination of their ride, for though it was a very delightful one, it was long, and the fact that the night was not dark made it seem longer even than it was. At least, so John thought. He said it seemed like two long days together, without any night between.

CHAPTER XV.

THE PRINCE CONSORT.

GRIMKIE and John had both been very curious to see how Wick would look, and they watched for the first appearance of it with great interest. It proved to be a small and ancient looking town, built very compactly of gray stone, and situated at the bottom of a small bay which here sets in from the sea. In front of it was a little port formed by two piers built out into the water, and curved in such a manner as to enclose a considerable space of smooth water, with a small opening between the two ends of them, to allow the fishing boats to pass in and out. As usual in such cases there was a light-house on the end of one of these piers.

"The very first thing we will do, Grimkie," said John, "will be to go down to the piers and see the fishing boats."

"After breakfast," said Grimkie.

It was now nearly noon and the party had had no breakfast, excepting some cakes and oranges which Grimkie had brought in his knapsack, and which they ate very early in the morning.

The coach drove rapidly into the town, and stopped at the door of a snug and neat-looking inn, where Grimkie soon engaged rooms and ordered breakfast. The weather was cool, too, and Mrs. Morelle requested the waiter to have a good fire made in their sitting-room. In half an hour the breakfast was ready, and about the same time all the members of the party, having in the meanwhile been occupied, in their several rooms, in making their toilet, were ready to eat it. Of course their appetites were very eager, and as the breakfast was an excellent one, consisting of fresh herring nicely fried, beef-steaks, eggs, hot rolls, toast, coffee with plenty of hot milk and cream, fresh butter, and other such niceties, they all enjoyed the repast exceedingly.

"What a nice thing a really good breakfast is," said Florence, "when we have waited long enough for it to get completely hungry."

Pretty soon after breakfast they all went out to take a walk to see the town, and the pier. They first walked along through the principal street, looking into the shops to see if there was anything new or curious in them which it would be well to buy as souvenirs. Then they went down to the water, in order to see the pier. It was rather to please the two boys that they did this, but still Mrs. Morelle was very willing to go, for she was curious to see what the accommodations were for going on board the steamer in case she should conclude to embark the next morning.

They found that the piers were each very wide. On the inside of the enclosure formed by them was a range of vessels and fishingboats, which were moored to rings, and massive piles, on the margin of the pier, and near them were cranes and other such fixtures used for discharging cargoes. Then came a broad space to land goods upon, and beyond a road for carts and wagons. All this was upon the top of the pier, and on the outside was a high parapet wall to protect the platform and roadway, above described, from the wind and the sea.

Thus in walking along the road-way upon the piers, one could see the fishing boats and vessels within the port, and witness all the operations going on there, but the view seaward was intercepted by the parapet wall.

Mrs. Morelle was well satisfied with the appearance of the port, and with the probable facilities for going on board the steamer, which she supposed would come inside, so as to allow the passengers to go on board by means of a broad plank.

The weather, too, was very fine, and she presumed that the sea was smooth. She had an opportunity soon of ascertaining this point, for on arriving at the end of one of the piers there were steps leading up to a lookout upon the top of the parapet wall, and she asked Grimkie to go up there and look out to sea, and make a report of the appearance of things.

Grimkie did so and reported that the surface of the water was smooth as glass, as far as he could see.

"Then," said she, "if there is no change before night we will go.

Mrs. Morelle and Florence soon returned to the hotel, but the boys spent most of the afternoon in rambling about the pier, examining the fishing boats, talking with the fishermen, and watching the various operations which were going on in the port. When they went home to tea, Grimkie asked what time the steamer would come the next morning, and the porter informed him that she was due about two o'clock, but that there was some uncertainty in respect to the time of her arrival. He said, however, that she would remain some hours at Wick, and that he would call them an hour before it would be time for them to go on board.

The whole party went to bed in good season,

both because they had so little sleep the night before, and also because they were to be called up so early the following morning.

It was about half-past one when the porter knocked at their doors to waken them. It was light enough to dress without candles, and they were all soon ready. When they came down to the door they found the porter there with a barrow. The baggage was put upon the barrow, and the porter set forward, followed by the party of travellers on foot. It was a bright and pleasant morning, and the air was calm. Mrs. Morelle was greatly pleased by the prospect before her.

After walking through several streets, they came to the pier but Mrs. Morelle looked in vain for the steamer.

"Why, Grimkie!" she exclaimed in surprise, "where is the steamer?"

"She must be out *there*," said Grimkie, pointing as he spoke to a column of smoke which was seen rising into the air over and beyond the parapet wall.

"And how are we going to get on board?" asked Mrs. Morelle.

"It must be that we are going in a boat," said Grimkie, "but you won't mind that, Auntie."

Mrs. Morelle saw at a glance that it was too late now to retreat, and she had the good sense to go forward boldly, acting upon the excellent principle, that when there is anything disagreeable before us which must be done, it is just as well to do it with a good grace.

Mrs. Morelle found, moreover, as we often do in such cases, that the difficulties which she anticipated disappeared as she approached them. At a certain part of the pier, not far from the entrance, there was a flight of stone steps leading down to the water. The boat which was to take the passengers to the steamer lay at the bottom of these steps. There was a small party of passengers immediately preceding Mrs. Morelle and her company. Seeing them go down at once, Mrs. Morelle followed, and all were soon safe on board the boat, seated in the stern. The trunks and other packages were then handed down and placed in the bows.

After waiting some little time for other passengers who were seen coming along the pier, the boat put off and was rowed easily out through the opening, and there the steamer came into full view. They were soon alongside of it, and without any difficulty ascended to the deck.

It was now nearly sunrise, but everything was

very quiet on board the steamer. The children seemed quite inclined to remain on deck to see what would take place, but Mrs. Morelle wished first to go below and find her berth or her stateroom. So they all went down.

They descended a short and winding stair-way, and at the bottom of it entered the cabin. On each side of the cabin, near the entrance to it, there was a row of three or four staterooms partitioned off, which made the cabin itself in this part, comparatively narrow. It was wide enough, however, for two long tables which stood here, with comfortable cushioned seats on each side of them.

Beyond the staterooms the cabin widened to the whole breadth of the ship, and was terminated toward the stern in a great semicircular sweep, with two tiers of wide and soft sofas, covered with crimson plush. The two tiers were parallel to each other, one above and back of the first, like the seats of an amphitheatre, and almost all the sofas were occupied by passengers, more or less covered with blankets and fast asleep. There were also some sleepers lying upon the sofas near the tables in the narrow part of the cabin. The sleepers seemed all to be men, except that there were one or two whose faces had a feminine expression, and Grimkie could not tell whether they were young women, or very pretty boys.

"Where is the ladies' cabin?" asked Mrs. Morelle, turning to the stewardess, who had met the party at the foot of the stairs and followed them into the cabin.

"Here it is, madam," said the stewardess. "But it is pretty full."

So saying, the stewardess led the way to a passage behind the stairs, and there, pulling aside a certain screen before a door, she disclosed a room in the sides of which were berths, and on the floor sofas, cots, and beds made of cushions, all of which were filled with female sleepers lying in all imaginable attitudes. Mrs. Morelle and Florence turned back immediately. It was evident that there was very little room for them there.

"Is not there any stateroom for us?" asked Mrs. Morelle.

"Oh yes," said the stewardess. And she at once led the way back to the main cabin, and there, opening one of the doors on the side, not far from the entrance, she ushered Mrs. Morelle and Florence into a very nice and bright-looking stateroom.

"Ah!" exclaimed Mrs. Morelle, the moment that she saw the interior of it, speaking in a tone of great satisfaction. "This is exactly what we want. Here is a berth for you and one for me. It is *exactly* what we want."

"I suppose there is something extra for the stateroom," she added, turning to the stewardess.

"Four shillings each," said the stewardess.

"We will take it," said Mrs. Morelle. "And as for you, boys, you must find places to sleep on the sofas in the cabin. We can't afford a stateroom for you."

"We don't *want* any stateroom, mother," said John. "I would a great deal rather sleep in the cabin."

So the boys went to the cabin, and all four of the party were soon in their several berths or upon their sofas sound asleep. The steamer was quiet and still, except the slight jarring sensation produced by the paddles after she began to move through the water, and the passengers all continued to sleep after this for several hours, for although it was near sunrise when Mrs. Morelle and her party came on board, still, in respect to the time for sleeping, it was not much past the middle of the night.

There began to be a movement for getting up in the gentleman's cabin about seven o'clock, and soon after this time Grimkie and John rose and went on deck. There they took out their maps and endeavored by calculation of the distance which they had run, and the bearing of the land which was in sight, to find out where they were.

One of the passengers who saw what they were doing, came and informed them that a certain large island which they were passing was Ronaldsay, one of the Orkneys, and that the land beyond it which extended in both directions as far as they could see, was another of the islands, and that the steamer would arrive at Kirkwall in about two hours. They found out the name of the steamer too,—the *Prince Consort.* She was named thus in honor of Prince, Albert, the consort of the queen.

The boys remained on deck watching the land as cape after cape and headland after headland came into view, for an hour more, and then Grimkie sent John down to knock at his mother's stateroom door, and tell her that they were drawing near to Kirkwall.

In about half an hour after receiving this summons, Mrs. Morelle and Florence came upon deck.

The steamer had turned in now among the islands, where the water was sheltered and smooth as in a river, and the views on every side were enchanting. The principal islands were so large that they looked like portions of the main land, and they presented an appearance of verdure and beauty impossible to describe. Great fields of the richest green, separated from each other by hedges neatly trimmed, or by substantial walls, extended in every direction as far as the eye could reach, while elegant villas, and spacious farm-houses, and rows of cottages appearing here and there, diversified the scene. The fields in many cases sloped down smoothly and beautifully to the water's edge. In other places the line of the coast was formed of rocky cliffs with the surf of the sea rolling in at the base of them, and far in the interior lofty mountains were seen marking their dim blue outline upon the sky.

"Well, Grimkie," said Mrs. Morelle, "what do you think of the Orkneys?"

"I don't think much of them," said Grimkie, with an air of disappointment. "The sea is as smooth, and the country is as beautiful, as any where in England. I don't believe the Norsemen had very hard times after all."

"Ah!" said Mrs. Morelle, "you ought to be here in January, when there is as little day as there is night now."

The cabin and the deck of the steamer was soon all in a bustle in consequence of the preparations which were made by the Orkney passengers to land. The steamer turned in more and more among the islands, until at last she approached Kirkwall, which was situated, like Wick, at the bottom of a small bay, and had a port formed of two piers for the protection of fishing boats and other small vessels. The steamer came to anchor outside this port. Boats came out to receive the passengers and their luggage. In these boats they were all conveyed within the port, and landed at a small pier sloping down to the water's edge.

Here a number of porters were assembled to take the luggage of the passengers into the town. There were no carriages. A group of islands is not the region in which carriages are likely to be multiplied. Grimkie selected from among the porters one who had an honest face, and giving him the trunk asked him to lead the way to the hotel. The porter went on into a very narrow street—the width of it being barely sufficient for a single carriage—between ancient stone buildings which had more the appearance of prisons than houses—so few were the windows, and so deep were they sunk into the massive walls—and thus they arrived at the hotel.

CHAPTER XVI.

KIRKWALL.

THE hotel at Kirkwall, when it first came into view, presented a very unpromising appearance. It was built upon a little paved court, the front, containing the entrance being at the back side of the court, and two wings one on each side extending forward to the street. A low wall, with two gateways through it, extended along the line of the street from one of these wings to the other.

The building itself, like all the buildings in the town, was formed of very thick and massive walls of stone, with windows set in so far back in the wall, that the sashes scarcely appeared in view. Indeed in looking along the street the windows of the houses appeared only as openings in the wall, as if the buildings were so many stone barns.

On entering the hotel, however, the scene was entirely changed. The waiter conducted the party up to the second story, and ushered them at once into a large and handsomely furnished room. There was a bright fire blazing in the grate, and a polished mahogany dining-table in the middle of the floor, and arm-chairs, and sofas, and carpets, and curtains to the windows, and tables in the corners covered with books, and stands of flower-pots with flowers in full bloom, and many other nameless conveniences and elegancies which are comprised in the idea of a comfortable parlor in an English inn.

"Ah, Florence!" exclaimed Mrs. Morelle. "This is just the place for us. How glad I am to see the fire. I did not know I was so cold."

The chambermaid came soon to show the ladies their chamber, and Mrs. Morelle when she went into hers, asked Grimkie to order the best breakfast that he could get for them. In half an hour the breakfast was ready, and very soon after breakfast the whole party set out to take a walk and see the town.

They found that the town consisted chiefly of a very long and narrow street, which followed the curvature of the shore. It was very narrow, and seemed intended almost exclusively for foot-passengers. There was only a narrow track in the center of it—about two feet wide, that is, just wide enough for one horse—that was paved like a street. The rest of the space on each side was covered with flag stones for foot-passengers. Thus the street was almost all sidewalk.

"We may know by the narrowness of the streets and by the looks of the houses that they have dreadful gales of wind and storms here in the winter," said Grimkie. "See what thick walls, and what little windows and how few! See how deep the windows are set in the walls, so that the gales may not get at them to burst them in!"

The party walked on for some time, following the windings of the street, and looking in at the shop windows to see what sort of things there were to sell. At one place they saw some views in the Orkneys, hanging at the window of a print shop. There was a view of some of the coast scenery, with lofty mountains rising abruptly out of the sea, and tremendous precipices. There was a view also of the town of Kirkwall, and one of Stromness, a place upon the opposite side of the island. But the picture which most attracted the attention of Mrs. Morelle and Florence, was one of the STONES OF STENNIS. It was a view of an open plain in a wild and desolate country, with a range of gigantic stones, like immense tombstones, set up in the ground.

"What is this?" asked Mrs. Morelle; "what are the stones of Stennis?"

"Ah, that is something very curious," replied Grimkie. "I read an account of them. They are on the road to Stromness. We must go to see them."

"They look like the pictures I have seen of Stonehenge," said Florence.

"They are like Stonehenge," said Grimkie.

After going along a little farther, the party came to a sort of open space in which there was an immense cathedral, old and ruinous, though it bore marks of having been recently repaired. Mrs. Morelle was much surprised to see this edifice. She wondered how there could ever have been any occasion for a structure of such magnitude in so remote a region, and still more how it could ever have been built. But the truth is that the earls of Orkney, who formerly ruled over the islands like sovereign princes, were at one time very wealthy and powerful, and there was a time moreover, during the period in which the Catholic religion was in the ascendency in these countries, when the cathedrals and abbeys, and monasteries which were built in the north of Scotland, and in the islands adjacent, were of the grandest and most gorgeous description.

"Would you like to go in and see the cathedral, Auntie?" asked Grimkie.

"Do they have service in it on Sunday?" rejoined Mrs. Morelle.

"In one end of it," said Grimkie. "One end is finished off for a church. The rest of it is empty."

"Then we shall see it to-morrow when we go to church," replied Mrs. Morelle, "and that will be better. I like to see such places better when the people are in them."

The stones with which the cathedral had been repaired were of a red color, which gave them the appearance of monstrous bricks. They were really of sandstone, though of a bright color. John said that he read in a guide book that they were obtained from a quarry in a cliff which was named Red Head.

Near the cathedral were the ruins of two ancient palaces, the bishop's and the earl's. These ruins were very ancient and venerable, and Mrs. Morelle and Florence were greatly interested in walking about them, and looking up to the ivy covered battlements and towers. It was melancholy to look upon these utterly abandoned ruins. The air of desolation and solitude which reigned around them was greater than Mrs. Morelle had ever observed in any ruins before. In England there are many remains of ancient edifices, but they are all objects of great interest to tourists, and are visited by great numbers of people, for whose benefit the grounds are kept in order, and a certain degree of life is imparted to the scene. But these old palaces seemed not only to have outlived their possessors and occupants, but to have been utterly forsaken and forgotten by all the world, and an air of solitude and desolation reigned around them that it would be impossible to describe.

After passing by the ruins of the palaces, Mrs. Morelle and the children found themselves coming out into the country at a place where the road ascended a hill. They concluded to continue their walk until they reached the summit, in order to take a survey of the situation of Kirkwall, and of the surrounding country. So they walked slowly on, stopping occasionally to look at objects of interest, or to talk with the peasant women whom they met in the road, or found standing at their cottage doors.

They asked one of these women about their mode of life in the winter. Among other questions they asked her if the days were not very short at that season of the year.

"Yes," said she, "very short. In fact there is not much of any day in the winter, and it is always snowing, or blowing, or raining, or something else, so that there is not much chance to work upon the land. So the men stay in the barns a great deal, and thrash the grain, and do other such things, by the light of lanterns."

"But I should think the ground would be frozen up in the winter," said Grimkie, "and that that would prevent working on the land."

"No," said the woman. "The ground does not freeze much. We can always work on the land when it is good weather."

"That's very strange," said Grimkie, "so far north as this."

"And is not the ground covered with snow?" asked Mrs. Morelle.

"Not much," said the woman. "It snows very often, but the snow does not lie on the ground much."

"And don't you travel in sleighs here in the winter then?" asked John.

"Sleighs?" repeated the woman, looking puzzled, "what are they?"

"Sledges perhaps you call them," suggested Mrs. Morelle.

"No," replied the woman. "We never use sledges. But they do in some countries I've heard tell."

After reaching the top of the hill, the party stopped to take a survey of the country around, and a very magnificent spectacle presented itself to view. The land extended in every direction farther than they could see, but it was divided and separated into so many portions by bays, straits, inlets, and channels formed by the sea, that the view exhibited as charming a combination of land and water as could possibly be imagined. The islands which were near were formed of green and fertile slopes of land, of marvelous beauty, with pretty dells and vales opening here and there among them, and hamlets and villages, and farm-houses, and gentlemen's seats, dotting the country in every direction. Toward the west ranges of lofty mountains were seen. Grimkie took out his map and a little pocket compass which he had, and endeavored to ascertain the names of some of the highest peaks, by the bearings and distances of them. He pointed out in what direction they would go in their ride to Stromness, and where the Stones of Stennis were,—though the spot was not actually in view, being concealed by an intervening mountain.

They saw great numbers of cattle and sheep feeding on the hill sides in every direction. Indeed cattle and sheep are the staple productions of the Orkney Islands. The climate is so wet that the grass grows luxuriantly, and notwithstanding the high latitude the air is so tempered by the influence of the surrounding seas that it continues green nearly all the year.

To the west and south, lofty mountains were seen, in the distance. Grimkie and John were greatly taken with the view of these mountains. They concluded that they must lie at the south of Stromness.

"When we go to Stromness we will go up to the top of them, Johnnie," said Grimkie.

John very readily assented to this proposal, and Florence said that they must take her too.

After remaining upon the top of the hill until they were satisfied with studying the localities which were in sight, and with admiring the different views, they all descended again, and returned to the hotel. Instead, however, of going back through the main street, they took another course which led them along the margin of the water. Here they saw the piers which formed the little port, and the fishing boats lying inside of them, and many other curious things. Among other objects that arrested their attention was a small hut near the shore, the roof of which was made of an old boat turned upside down. The boat was supported by walls of stone which formed the sides of the hut, and there was a door in front to go in by. John was so much pleased with this curious hut that he took paper and a pencil out of his pocket in order to draw it, and he remained behind, to make his sketch, while the rest of the party went on ; so that he did not return to the hotel until some time after the others arrived.

He had, however, made a very pretty drawing —so pretty that Florence asked him to copy it in ink in her journal book, which John readily promised to do.

CHAPTER XVII.

THE STONES OF STENNIS.

Mrs. Morelle and her party remained many days at the Orkney Islands, and during this time they made a number of excursions, some in a carriage and some on foot. The only carriage, however, which they could obtain was a dog-cart, which was anything but a comfortable vehicle for ladies going out upon an excursion for pleasure. Indeed Florence expressed the opinion, that however well adapted it might be for the conveyance of dogs, it was the worst contrived vehicle for human beings that she ever saw. The only redeeming quality which it possessed was that in case it rained one umbrella would cover the whole company—after a fashion.

In this dog-cart they went to visit the Stones of Stennis. The road was most excellent all the way, being macadamized in a most perfect manner, so that it was as smooth as a gravel walk in a gentleman's park. The country, however, through which it passed, after a few miles from Kirkwall, was an almost boundless expanse of moorland, wild and desolate. After going on for some miles through this dreary country, the carriage left the main road and passed by a sort of cart track through the fields and over a long causeway between two lakes, till it came to the place where the stones were situated.

The stones could be seen for a distance of many miles, standing like so many gigantic posts on a vast plain. When the party came to the spot, they found that each stone was from twelve to twenty feet high, and about five feet wide and one thick. They were of a somewhat irregular form, being evidently slabs taken from the natural strata in the neighborhood, and set up just as they came from the quarry. They were arranged in an immense circle with the remains of an embankment and ditch all around the circumference. The circle was not complete, the stones being wanting in many places. In some cases they had fallen and still remained upon the ground. In other places where it would seem stones must have stood, the fragments had been taken away, it was supposed, after they had fallen, to be used for buildings or walls, by generations that lived in ages subsequent to that in which the stones were set up, but which have still in their turn long since passed away.

A great many conjectures have been made in

respect to these stones, and to the nature of the structure of which they formed a part, but all is uncertainty in respect to them. At the very earliest periods of which there is any account of the country, they stood as they stand now, solitary and in ruin—an inexplicable wonder to all who saw them.

The party went also to Stromness, a town at the western side of the island on which Kirkwall stands, and here, while Mrs. Morelle and Florence remained at the inn, Grimkie and John engaged a sail boat and a man to manage it, and made a cruise of four or five hours along the neighboring shores. There they saw some stupendous cliffs, called the Black Craigs, and great numbers of birds flying about them, and among other birds they saw an eagle perched upon a lofty summit, where he stood silent and solitary, looking far and wide over the sea. Grimkie and John had an excellent view of him through their opera glass.

At one time while the party remained at Kirkwall, they were imprisoned nearly a whole day by a pouring rain. Mrs. Morelle, when she found, as she did after breakfast, that there was no prospect that any of them could go out, asked the waiter if they had any books in the hotel relating to the Orkney Islands. The

THE BLACK CRAIGS.

waiter said he would inquire, and pretty soon he came in bringing a number of books of different sizes, some old and some new; some with pictures in them and some without. Mrs. Morelle directed that a good fire should be made, and the table cleared, and then placed these books upon the table and said that she was going to have a school.

"We will begin at ten o'clock," said she. "You can take your seats at the table, or at the windows, or where you please, and for two hours we will all look over these books and see how much we can learn about the Orkneys. Then we will have a luncheon. After luncheon we will each of us take a sheet of paper and a pen and ink and write down the most interesting thing that we have learned."

This plan was entered into by all the children very cordially. They spent two hours in studying the books and looking at the pictures. Then came the luncheon which consisted of some slices of cold roast mutton very tender and nice, with some flat rolls of bread, sweet fresh butter, strawberry preserves and cold coffee.

After the luncheon all spent an hour in writing, and by that time it had stopped raining. So it was concluded to postpone reading the compositions until the evening.

In the evening they were read. Florence's was as follows:

"THE POISONED SHIRT.

"In former times there was an earl of Orkney, named Hacon. He married a wife and had a son named Paul. After this his wife died, and then he married a princess of Caithness, named Helga.

"Caithness is the northern part of Scotland. It was a kingdom in those days, now it is a county.

"After his second marriage Hacon had another son named Harold.

"Harold and his mother hated Paul because he was the oldest son, and was entitled to the succession, and they did all in their power to supplant him in his father's affections. They succeeded so far that the old king finally agreed that Paul should not have the whole kingdom, but should share it with Harold. Accordingly, when the old king died the two sons were joined in the government of the islands.

"But they did not agree together at all. Helga was continually maneuvering with her son Harold to gain for him more than his share of the power. At length the two brothers came to open war, and the whole country was desolated by their dreadful fights.

"At last, after becoming weary of this, they agreed to make a treaty, and become reconciled, and as a pledge of the reconciliation, it was agreed that after the ratification of the treaty, each brother should invite the other to a grand feast, about the time of Christmas.

"When it came to Paul's turn to be invited to Harold's feast, Helga, the mother, determined to poison him. Her plan was to make a beautiful embroidered garment for him, as a present, in token of her entire reconciliation to him, and then before giving him the garment to poison it, so that it should kill him when he put it on. She kept this plan a profound secret from all but a sister who was living with her, named Franquart, to whom she confided her design. Franquart aided her in embroidering the garment, and in applying the poison.

At length, on the morning of the feast, Harold, happening to come into his mother's room, saw the beautiful garment lying there, all ready to be given to Paul when he should arrive, and asked what it was. His mother told him that it was a present that she and Franquart had been making for Paul. Harold was much enraged to hear this, and said that he would not allow of their offering Paul handsomer presents than they made for him. So he seized the garment and declared that he would keep it for himself. His mother and Franquart were dreadfully alarmed. They begged and implored him to put the garment down. But they could not tell him that it was poisoned without betraying their own guilt. In the end Harold went away with the garment, leaving his mother and Franquart, in the utmost distress and terror.

"Harold immediately put on the garment, and he died that very night in great agony.

"The consequence was that Paul regained his whole kingdom, and when he discovered the treachery which Helga and Franquart had attempted to practice upon him, he drove them out of the islands."

Grimkie's composition was as follows:

"THE EAGLE AND THE BABY.

"In one of the Orkney Islands named Hoy, where there are a great many high mountains and lofty precipices near the sea, there lived a fisherman named Halco. He had a small hut on the rocks, and a boat. There was a little green spot near his hut where he used to dry his nets, and where his little child, whose name was

Halco too, used to lie sometimes, and roll in the grass, and play.

"There are a great many eagles among the rocks of Hoy, and they often carried off the farmers' lambs, but as Halco had no sheep or lambs he did not pay much attention to the eagles.

"One day when Halco was coming home in his boat, just before he reached the shore he saw a monstrous eagle hovering over his hut, and after wheeling round and round several times in the air, he made a fell swoop toward the ground, and disappeared behind the hut. A moment afterward Halco saw him come up again, and to his amazement and horror he saw that he had little Halco in his claws.

"The eagle rose slowly with the child, and passing directly over Halco's head soared to a great height, and then sailed away to his nest on the summit of a cliff.

"Halco was almost stupefied by the terrible shock which he had received. He pulled like a madman to get to the shore. When he entered his hut he found his wife in a swoon. He paid no attention to her but seized his gun and rushed out of the hut. He climbed up the mountain side, and after great labor he came near enough to the nest to see the eagle perched upon the edge of it. He crept up a little nearer, and then took aim and fired. The eagle, after balancing and tottering a moment on his perch, fell heavily over, down the face of the cliff, and disappeared. Halco climbed out to the place of the nest, and there he found his little child, safe and sound, and playing with the young eagles."

"Why, Grimkie!" said John, as soon as Grimkie had finished reading his narrative, "I found a story a little like that, about an eagle carrying off a child, but there was not half as much in it as you have told."

"I thought I would embellish it a little," said Grimkie. "I presume it is just as true after I embellished it, as it was before."

John's composition was very short. It was as follows :

"THE HOLE IN THE STONE.

"In one of the stones of Stennis, is a round hole passing directly through the stone, not far from the edge. Nobody knows what this hole was made for by the people who set up the stone, but for a great many ages past it has been considered sacred for engagements. Whenever two persons wish to make any solemn agreement they go to Stennis and put their hands through this hole, and clasp them together in the center of it and then make the promise. If they do this they consider themselves solemnly bound.

"Lovers used to do this when they engaged themselves to each other. And it is said they do so now sometimes. Grimkie and I wanted to try it, but we could not think of anything to promise each other."

Instead of a composition Mrs. Morelle wrote a letter to America, giving an account of the journey and voyage to the Orkney Islands. She read this letter to the children after they had finished reading their compositions, and then, though it was yet very light, they all went to bed.

CHAPTER XVIII.

THE EMBARKATION.

AFTER remaining for some time in the islands, and making many excursions, sometimes by land and sometimes by water, in one of which Grimkie and John went out in one of the fishing boats, and had an excellent time fishing, the party began to look forward with some interest to the time for setting out on their return. The question arose *how* they should return. John was very eager to go by the mail boat across the Pentland Firth, instead of returning by the steamer, as they came.

The steamer made the trip only once a week. It started from Edinburgh, touched at Aberdeen and at Wick, then, after going to Kirkwall in the Orkneys, proceeded to the Shetland Islands, sixty miles or more farther north. Then returning by the same way, she went back to Edinburgh. This voyage, with the necessary detentions at the different ports, occupied six days, so that there was no opportunity of returning to

Scotland by the *Prince Consort*, except once a week.

It was necessary to send the mail to the Orkneys, however, every day, and John had found out that a special service had been organized for this purpose over the islands toward the south by some sort of mail-cart, and thence across the Pentland Firth, at the narrowest place, to the coast of Scotland, in a sail boat. Thence by coach or mail-cart to Wick, and so south toward England.

There were three reasons why John wished to go by this route. First, he wished to see what sort of travelling riding in a mail cart would be. Next he had a great desire to see the Pentland Firth, and to cross it in a sail boat. He had heard wonderful accounts of this famous channel—of the furious tides and currents that swept through it, producing whirlpools, and boiling surges, and roaring breakers of the most wonderful character, and he was very curious to see them. Then, lastly, by this route he had hoped to go and see John O'Groat's house.

John O'Groat's house, the name of which has become so famous all the world over, stands, or rather stood, upon the very extremity of Scotland, toward the northeast, and as the opposite corner of the island toward the southwest, is called Land's End, there arose the expression from the Land's End to John O'Groat's, to denote the whole territory of Great Britain.

But inasmuch as the British territory extended to the southwest to several islands the most remote of which in that direction is Jersey, and as it also includes on the north the Shetland Islands, the most northern point of which is called Ska, the expression would more fully comprehend all that is intended, if instead of being "from Land's End to John O'Groat's," it was "from Jersey to Ska."

The story of John O'Groat is, that he had six relatives or friends who when they came to see him quarreled in respect to which should take precedence in going out at the door, and in order to settle the question, he built a six-sided house, with a door in each side, and made a six-sided table within, with a side toward each door, so that each of his guests might have a seat of honor, and seem to be first in going out when the feast was over.

John O'Groat's house is now nothing but a name, as all traces of the building—if any such ever existed—have long since disappeared. Nothing marks the spot but a little green mound, which tradition says is the one which the building formerly occupied.

The Embarkation.

It was found on inquiry, that John's plan for returning to Scotland, was wholly impracticable. It was very inconvenient and very expensive, for a single individual to go by the mail route, over the islands and across the firth, but for a party as large as Mrs. Morelle's, it was impossible. There was no alternative but to take the steamer.

"We must take the steamer, too, whatever the weather is," said. Mrs. Morelle, "unless we are willing to remain here another whole week, with the chance of finding worse weather still at the end of it."

In fact, however, when the morning arrived for expecting the *Prince Consort* on her return from Shetland, the weather proved to be very fine. The steamer was expected to come into port at eight o'clock, and to remain there several hours.

"So that you need be in no hurry," said the porter, who gave Grimkie this information. "You can take your breakfast quietly, and then go on board at your leisure. The steamer will not sail before eleven or twelve."

"Why does she remain here so long?" asked Grimkie.

"It takes some time to get the cattle on board," said the porter. "You see they have to take them all out in boats, and then get them on board."

"Cattle!" exclaimed John. "Do the cattle go a sailing in the steamboat?"

"Oh yes," said the porter, smiling, "great numbers of them. There's no other way to get the cattle, and sheep, and other animals, that are raised on these islands to market. They can't get to England by land, and so the steamer takes them. That is the main business of the steamer in fact."

As soon as Grimkie and John heard this they were both eager to go on board the steamer as soon as possible after she came into port, as they were extremely desirous of witnessing the operation of getting cattle and horses up to her deck from a boat out in the middle of the harbor.

"In the first place," said John, "I don't see how they'll get them into the boats—and then when they get the boats to the side of the steamer, I can't imagine how they are going to make them go up such a steep and narrow ladder."

John had seen no other mode of ascending and descending to the deck of the steamer, from boats alongside, but by the step-ladder used by the passengers, and he did not think of there being any other mode.

Grimkie, with Mrs. Morelle's consent, ordered breakfast at half past seven, and he told the porter that they should wish to go on board as soon as the steamer came in. Mrs. Morelle had no objection to this, for they knew that the steamer being in harbor, would be at rest, and though they expected to have to wait on board for several hours they thought that they should be likely to find more to amuse them there during that time than at the hotel, where they had become entirely familiar with every thing that was to be seen.

Grimkie and John also took pains to have every thing packed and ready before the breakfast came upon the table, so that they might be all prepared to go on board immediately after breakfast, in case the steamer should arrive so soon. It was not, however, till about nine o'clock that the porter came to call them.

There are no cabs or hackney coaches of any kind in the Orkneys, and so every body walks to the landing when they are going on board the steamer. When the time arrived the porter came for the trunk, and steadying the trunk on his shoulder with one hand, and carrying the night valise in the other, he led the way out through the court of the hotel. As soon as they entered the street, Mrs. Morelle and Florence were both alarmed at the sight of a monstrous bull, which a man was leading before them, and which was followed by a troop of men and boys.

"Let us go slowly," said she, "till that bull gets out of the way."

"I verily believe he is going on board the steamer," said Grimkie.

"No," said John; "It can't be. They might possibly get him into a boat and row him out there, but if they think that they can get such a fellow as that up that little narrow black stepladder, they will find themselves very much mistaken I can tell them. *I* know more about bulls than that, myself."

Mrs. Morelle did not gain much advantage by keeping back and walking slowly, for when at length she reached the landing place, she found the bull standing there surrounded by people. There were also some curious-looking boxes there, of the form of stalls for cattle, but Mrs. Morelle did not stop to look at them, being in haste to go past the bull and get into the boat. She effected this object safely. A number of other passengers went on board the boat at the same time. Their luggage was also put in, and then the boatmen pushed off, and rowed out to the steamer.

Mrs. Morelle and Florence, who were beginning to be somewhat accustomed to going on

THE EMBARKATION. 241

board a steamer from a boat, found no difficulty in going up the step-ladder, however difficult such a feat might be expected to prove for a bull. As for the boys, they liked much better embarking in this way than to walk over a plank from a pier. As soon as they were all on board they went below to choose a stateroom for the two ladies. Mrs. Morelle offered also to take a stateroom for the boys, but they preferred to be in the cabin they said, so as to see and hear what was going on.

As soon as the stateroom was chosen they all went up to the deck again, and after Grimkie and John had found seats for Mrs. Morelle and Florence, where they could see all around, and especially on the side toward the little port, where sail boats and fishing boats were continually coming and going, John took the opera glass, and began to watch the boats as they came in succession out from the opening between the two piers, which formed the entrance to the port, in order to see when the bull came, if he could.

After scrutinizing a number of boats, which proved to be only fishing boats going out to sea, or passage boats belonging to private individuals going away to some of the other islands, John saw a very broad and heavy boat coming propelled by oars. After gazing at it a moment with great attention through his glass, he exclaimed, in a very excited manner,

"Yes, Grimkie! he is coming! Here he is! I can see his horns!"

Then after a moment's pause he added,

"There are a great many of them,—bulls and oxen, or something. I can see a great many horns. Look! Grimkie. Look!"

So saying, he gave Grimkie the glass, and by the time Grimkie had got the boat into the field of view it had come so much nearer that he could see very plainly that it was very large and that it had a sort of floor in the bottom of it which was completely filled with oxen and cows. The animals stood together as close as they could be packed, and Grimkie could just see their heads and necks above the gunwales of the boat.

"I don't understand how they got them into that boat," said John, "and we will see pretty soon how they make out in driving them up this little stair."

"They won't drive them up there," said Grimkie. "That is the gangway for the passengers. They won't take them into this part of the steamer at all."

"Where will they take them in then?" asked John.

"Forward," said Grimkie.

"Then let us go forward and see," said John.

"Very well," said Grimkie. "This is the way."

There was a broad bridge extending across from one paddle-wheel to the other, at some distance above the main deck, and a walk, with railings on each side, extending fore and aft from this bridge to the quarter deck where Mrs. Morelle and Florence were sitting. The boys went along the walk to the bridge, and there, as they looked down upon the forward deck, an extraordinary spectacle met their view. The space was divided into pens,—made by small iron posts set up in the deck, and strong bars connecting them—and these pens were filled with animals of all kinds, cows, sheep, horses, ponies, oxen, and even pigs. These animals had all been taken on board at Shetland,—the produce of the farms there, which the farmers were sending to market.

Among all these animals those which most attracted the attention of the boys, were the Shetland ponies. They stood together in a pen by themselves. They were of various sizes, and although they all had the general form and appearance of the horse, some of them were very small. There was one that John said would be *too* small even for *him*.

These ponies were going to England to be sold there to gentlemen who were willing to buy them for their boys, to ride about upon over the smooth gravel roads made in their parks and pleasure-grounds. Such ponies are used too by ladies to drive over the same kind of roads in a small and light open chaise, called a pony-chaise.

Before the boys had satisfied themselves with looking at the ponies, their attention was suddenly called away by the arrival of the boat-load of cows, which now came up alongside of the steamer at a place where an opening had been made in the bulwarks for the purpose of taking them in. They immediately went over to that side of the steamer, and looked down from their elevated position upon the bridge, to watch the mode of proceeding for getting the cattle on board.

Just beneath them was an iron crane with a small steam engine attached to it, by which it was worked. The whole was upon a small round iron platform, which moved upon a pivot in the deck, in such a manner that the platform could turn in any direction, carrying with it crane, engine, and all. There was a boy upon this platform who governed its motions by two polished iron handles which were connected with the different steam pipes. The boy received his orders from the men who had the management of the cattle, pulling and pushing his handles in different ways, according as they called out, *Lower! Hoist! Stop! Turn!*

There were two men in the boat with the cattle, crowding their way about among them, without paying the least attention either to their horns or their heels. The people from the deck threw down two broad bands, made of canvas or sail cloth, to these men. The men took one of the bands and passed it under one the cows, between her fore legs and her hind legs, and then brought the edges together over her back. In the meantime the boy had been called upon to "lower," and he turned his handles in such a way as to swing the top of the crane out over the boat and to lower the chain, which had a hook in the end of it, until the men in the boat could reach it and hook it into certain rings in the upper edges of the canvas over the cow's back.

The order was then given to the boy to "hoist," and immediately afterward the little steam engine began rapidly to wind up the chain whereupon the poor cow found herself suddenly lifted off from her feet, and rising rapidly into the air, her legs hanging down in the most awkward and helpless condition imaginable. As soon as she was raised fairly above the level of the deck, the men waiting there seized her by the head and horns and swung her in on board, and then the boy lowered her until her feet touched the planks, when she immediately began to spring and scramble to get away. At the same time instant the broad belt by which she had been lifted was dropped, and fell upon the deck and the cow was free. The men led her away by means of a short cord fastened to one of her horns, and put her in a pen with the other cattle.

By this process the cows were all hoisted out of the boat and landed upon the steamer, in a rapid and unceremonious manner. While one cow was coming up, the men in the boat were placing the second band under another one, so as to be ready to hook the chain to her, the moment it came down, and thus not a moment was lost. The words Lower, Hoist, Stop, Turn, followed each other in very rapid succession, and the little piston-rod of the engine plied its strokes in the nimblest possible manner, as cow after cow came up, until at length the boat was wholly cleared.

By the time that the first boat was empty another one came. This second one contained the bull, but instead of being free as the cows had been, he was secured fast in one of the moveable stalls which Mrs. Morelle had seen at the landing The stall was a narrow box, just wide enough for the bull to stand in it. It had a floor, two sides, two ends, but no top. Instead of a top, there were two irons passing over from one side to the other, above, giving the box the appearance of a monstrous oblong pail with two bails to it. When the chain was lowered the hooks were attached to these two bails, and the box, bull and all, was run up rapidly to the deck, and placed there in a secure position among the piers.

As fast as the remaining cattle were brought up, new pens were made upon the deck, and when at length the pens were all full, the hatches were opened, and a great many cows, after being hoisted up from the boat and swung round over the hatchways, were lowered down into the hold, to some dark and dismal region there, which the boys could not see.

Besides the cows and a load of oxen, there was a boat full of sheep that came on board, and also one of pigs. The pigs were hoisted two at a time—each of them having a band passed round him, and the hook taking hold of the rings of each band. The pigs made a frightful outcry at being hoisted in this manner.

There were a great many boxes containing fish, and packages of wool, and bags of grain, and other such things, the produce of the islands, that were also taken on board. The work of getting all the cargo in, and on board, occupied several hours, and it was near noon before the steamer was ready to sail.

CHAPTER XIX.

CONCLUSION.

THE sea was very smooth, and the air calm, on the day that Mrs. Morelle and her party made the voyage back from the Orkneys to what may be called in relation to them, the main land. Mrs. Morelle and Florence having some misgivings in respect to the effect which the sea might produce upon them, thought it best to remain below, at least until the steamer should arrive at Wick, because they could lie down while they were below, and a horizontal position is found to be the best means, both for guarding against the approach of sea-sickness, and for alleviating the sufferings produced by it when it comes.

"But we will not go into our stateroom, Grimkie," said Mrs. Morelle. "We will lie down upon the sofas in the great cabin, and then if we can not read we can amuse ourselves with observing what is going on."

Grimkie accordingly accompanied his aunt and cousin below, and found nice sofas for them there. He put two or three soft cushions at the head of each sofa, and when Mrs. Morelle and Florence had come down, he spread shawls over their feet, and gave them their books. Then leaving them to themselves he went upon deck again to join John.

Grimkie and John remained upon the deck all the afternoon, except that from time to time they went below to see if the ladies were doing well in the cabin. They watched the different islands as the steamer passed along their shores on her way to the southward, identifying them one after another by means of the map. When at length they came opposite to the Pentland Firth, John looked in that direction long and earnestly to see if he could discern any signs of the whirlpools, or foaming breakers that he read accounts of in the books,—but excepting a white line of surf which often appeared along the rocky shores at the margin of the water, nothing was to be seen.

In the meantime the coast of Caithness, the northern part of Scotland, had come fully into view, and presently the steamer, drawing nearer and nearer to the coast began to follow the line of it, at a little distance in the offing, toward Wick.

The steamer remained several hours at Wick, and the boys were at first very anxious to go on shore during the interval, but Mrs. Morelle thought it not prudent for them to do so. They afterward concluded, however, that they liked quite as well to remain on board, for a great many boat loads of cattle, sheep, and other animals were brought out and hoisted on board, and they were very much entertained in watching the operations.

At length, about nine o'clock in the evening, the steamer sailed again, and now her course led her out quite into the open sea, as will appear by an inspection of the map, which shows a great bay entering into the land between Wick and Aberdeen, across the mouth of which the track of the steamer lay. Mrs. Morelle and Florence determined to go into their stateroom at once, and go to bed, hoping to sleep during the whole time of passing across this bay. Grimkie and John remained on deck till eleven o'clock, and then, though it was still very light, they went below and took their places on the couches or sofas where Mrs. Morelle and Florence had lain during the afternoon, and were both soon sound asleep. They slept without any intermission until morning.

After this brief and prosperous voyage the whole party landed safely in Scotland, which seemed to them like a continent in comparison with the smaller islands that they had been to visit. There was a railway station very near the quay, and after spending a few hours at the hotel to take breakfast, and to rest a little from the voyage, they took places in the train for Perth and Edinburgh, and set out upon their journey about ten o'clock. They met with a great many entertaining adventures on the way toward London, but they can not be related in this volume.

THE END.

CPSIA information can be obtained
at www.ICGtesting.com
Printed in the USA
BVHW041453270622
640741BV00004B/235